Living Under the Shadow

Elizabeth Manning-Ives

To Gina
Best Wishes
EMI

Living Under the Shadow

Published by Woodlark Publishing
Copyright © Elizabeth Manning-Ives2015
ISBN-13: 9780993349102
ISBN-10: 0993349102

Acknowledgements

Grateful Thanks to:

Arthur Hyde for allowing me to use his painting for the cover of this book.

Lorraine Bennett for all her hard work and assistance in preparing this book for publication.

Catherine Quinlan for encouraging me to believe in myself.

Suzan Collins for all her help, support and encouragement throughout the writing and production of this book, as well as the Get Writing workshops which got me started.

Richard and Gina at the Coconut Loft in Lowestoft for their welcome, and for providing excellent cake.

Cover creation: Jen Moon

Dedication

This book is dedicated
to Alan and Andy

Part one

The hills that surround our tiny village are shrouded with mist; the tops are obscured by heavy grey clouds. This atmosphere makes the trade of our village even more sinister. As young children we never knew what our father was involved in, only that his work was done at night and we were never to ask any questions. As time went on mother became ill, and father became more and more controlling. Life is hard. As a girl I am not considered worthy of an education of any sort. Our mother was however educated as a child, she secretly gives me her own precious books, which I am teaching myself to read by candlelight when father is not at home. If he ever catches me then I am in trouble, all I want is to escape, to get away from this place, now it looks as if I am going to be trapped here for a long time to come.

I am Flora. The oldest of three children, although I was not the first born. I did have an older sister called Nettie whom I loved dearly, but she died two years ago aged just fourteen years eight months. I was only just thirteen at the time, Jasper was ten and Gertie only six. But my life was mapped out from that day. My one good friend Meg was the only person I could turn to then, and apart from mother she still is. She lives very close to us but we don't see each other very often, as we both have very controlling fathers, as well as younger siblings to help care for. Meg's father, Seth does have a paid job as a game-keeper, although he spends most of his time with my father Silas, helping with his work at night. The best chance Meg and I have of spending time together is late in the evening after the young ones are in bed, after our fathers have gone for the night, although since mother got sick these times have become so much fewer. Meg's mother has good health, so often allows us to meet in their house; in return we keep an eye on Agnes and Ned, while Meg's mother Hattie visits my house to assist my increasingly ailing, mother Martha. Agnes and Ned are twins, they are only just six, so cannot be left. Our meetings have to be pre-arranged and are not as often as either we, or our mother's, would like them to be but they give both of us a glimmer of light in our very dark, often fearful lives. Very occasionally we can take a walk together instead of baby sitting at Meg's house, but we are always told where we are allowed to walk and how long we are allowed to be. When we ask why we are always given the same answer, `take it or leave it, ask no more, just know it is for your own protection.' In recent days though, we have started to think that our fathers are beginning to suspect something. Neither father approves of our friendship, both telling us regularly that our place is at home not roaming the countryside. Meg and I want more out of life; we continually make plans, helping each other with reading and writing during our rare times together. The knowledge that our mother's support us in this venture is valuable, although they never say so in front of their husbands for fear of being beaten. We will also be beaten by our fathers if they find out. Beatings have become a regular occurrence in both families, especially when the men get drunk, which is at least three or four, times a week.

***

At last winter's grip has faded, hope is slowly returning as the promise of better weather is obvious in all of nature's changing beauty. A clear blue sky is above me; I am surrounded by the warm spring sunshine which is cooled by a playful breeze dancing through the trees. Birds chatter tunefully, the leaves seem to be whispering in response to the hum of bees lazily buzzing from flower to flower. This day should be perfect but my mind keeps returning to what lies ahead. Ever since mother moved to this village as a child she has known there is a darkness that hangs and lingers over it, though she would never tell me what it was. But only two weeks ago Meg and I stumble upon this sinister secret.

We were returning home late one evening, when what appeared to be horse's hooves could be heard in the distance, only they sounded muffled. Then ahead of us lamps were glowing, gruff, deep voices could be heard, not clearly as the men were almost whispering, but as we drew closer we felt very uneasy. Then before either of us knew what was happening the lights were extinguished, the voices stopped, a familiar odour filled the air. Tobacco smoke; I knew it at once, as father always has a pipe on the go.

Seconds passed before both of us felt a large rough hand firmly placed over our mouths and an arm tightly round our waists. Terror flooded through us like a river, nothing was said, and we did not know where each other were or what was happening. Who were these men? What were they going to do with us? They did not take us far before we entered a dimly lit, musty smelling building. No-one spoke until the door was locked and bolted. Hearts pounding, barely able to breathe, but relieved that we had not been separated Meg and I clung to each other, gaining a little solace in the knowledge that we were still together. Then I heard it, the familiar gruff voice of my own father, telling me he was in charge of a gang of smugglers, and that now we knew, Meg and I were to help in this trade or else.

So tonight is the night, our first time as lookouts. We are both terrified knowing that if the gang gets caught we are guilty too. If we get caught we will be expected to help the customs people in exchange for our lives. Smuggling is punishable by hanging; we are just as guilty as my father, even though we have no choice. My mother is too sick and ill to help; we are poor so father says there is no other way to put food on the table. I feel sick to my stomach just thinking about what I am about to do. Is there no way out for us? Can no-one help? Is this what my life is to be from now on? Only time will tell!

***

Meg and I have been working as lookouts for my father's smuggling ring for two months now and things at home are getting harder all the time. Father and I barely speak, and mother is now so weak, she is confined to her bed. Jasper, now twelve, and Gertie, only just eight, do what they can to help, but Gertie is too young to do much and Jasper being a boy is forbidden by our father to help with domestic chores. His eyesight is not good so he can't be used as a lookout. As yet neither of my siblings know anything about the smuggling, or at least I haven't burdened them with that knowledge because I still hope to make things better for them, even if I can't escape, I plan to help them to as soon as I can.

At the age of fifteen I know what it means when I am told that mother does not have long for this world. I feel as if my whole life is falling apart. Losing her will mean I have no-one to talk to, and as the oldest girl will be expected to assume my mother's role performing the necessary duties that go with it, not that I haven't been doing this for some time anyway. My chance of escaping this life seems to be slipping away, I can see no future, or escape for myself, Jasper or Gertie. This is my biggest concern.

As the days pass mother continues to get weaker, sleeping more than she is awake. Throughout all this I rarely leave her side, the love we feel for each other is stronger than it has ever been; only intensifying the hurt and desperation I feel.

This afternoon I am sitting beside my mother secretly reading one of my beloved books, a different feeling is filling the room. There is a heaviness and growing sense of dread inside me which I have not experienced before, as hard as I try I don't seem to be able to concentrate on my book at all. Then a very weak voice brings me back to reality with a jolt, mother hasn't spoken in days, why now? What does this mean?

`What is it mother? Don't try to speak you are too weak and must rest.'

Without another word she hands me a small white envelope. My poor frail mother falls back onto the pillow, instantly sleeping again. Trembling with fear, tears burning at the back of my eyes I stare at the envelope, but do not recognise the name upon it. Confused and uncertain I look around the room for anything that might shed a light on what has just been given to me. Slowly I move back towards the bed, I notice a tiny piece of paper on the floor beside the chair that I had been sitting on. Where had this come from? The envelope was sealed. Picking it up I begin to read the words written on it, a list of instructions. With tears now streaming down my face, I return to my mother's bedside. She is no longer breathing, her life has slipped away while I was trying to make sense of the strange instructions, I should have been with her, holding her hand. She should not have died alone; I cannot forgive myself for this, it's just not fair.

***

A week has passed since mother died, today we say goodbye to her as we attend her funeral and she is laid to rest. Jasper and Gertie are frightened and distraught. I don't know how to help them because I am feeling the same, as well as being weak with my own guilt. Father has barely acknowledged the

12

death of his wife, in fact he almost seems angry at her for dying, leaving him with three children. He is making us feel as if we are the cause of all his problems. The beatings are getting worse, especially for me.

The instructions which I had found the day mother died, told me to send the envelope immediately, this I had done. Though I still did not know what was really happening, or who the person was to whom the letter was sent.

***

Weeks have passed, my grief deepens by the day, but I can't let it show in front of father because I will be beaten. I carry out my chores in a blur trying my best to support Jasper and Gertie through their grief, but feeling desperate, knowing I can't keep it up for much longer. On top of it all, I am still expected to act as a lookout on a nightly basis for father and his smuggling ring.

Something has to change and fast. I am sitting at the kitchen table on this late summer afternoon resting my head on my arms, staring into space. I just feel so numb, all hope has left me. I have not been able to see Meg once since we buried mother. I am missing her friendship and support, but our meetings are now impossible.

The sound of horse's hooves coming along the road wakes me from a fitful but exhaustion induced sleep. Hurriedly I get up to look out of the window, but there is a loud knock at the door before I can even straighten my hair. I answer the door, to a well-dressed, well-spoken young man, with a kind but strangely familiar face, in his hand he is clutching the same small white envelope that mother had given to me moments before she died.

`Miss Flora I assume? '

Trembling all over, with a lump in my throat,

`Yes' I answer weakly.

What is happening? What does this young man want with me? And why has he got my mother's letter? Fear grips my whole being, I do not understand what all this means but I am fairly sure my whole life and that of my brother and sister is about to be turned upside down again. Except that this time, I have a feeling it will be in a very different way from before. Could this young man be the key to unlocking the life I have been yearning for my whole life? I don't know, but I already feel that he can be trusted, so I invite him into our ramshackle dwelling, ready to hear what he has to say.

`Miss Flora, my name is Thomas Havergal; I am the son of your late mother's cousin Lord Sebastian Havergal and his wife Lady Phoebe. It is with great sadness that my father received your mother's letter as he knew immediately what it meant. My grandfather did your grandmother and mother a great wrong many years ago. My father always kept in touch with your mother desperate to make amends for his father's actions. Now at last he feels that he can. Your mother would never leave you three children with your father because she knew his temper would be taken out on you particularly Flora, but in her letter she asks that you all be taken from here as soon as possible after her death, so you can be given the chance of a better life. This can only happen with your consent, when all the arrangements have been made. Before anything else happens I must return to my parents' home with your agreement that you will follow me when we send for you.'

`My agreement you have kind sir, but are my brother and sister to come too?' I ask hardly believing what I have just heard.

`Yes though not immediately, they will be safe for a while, you are in the most danger Flora. You will come to us with a new name; Silas will not be able to hurt you anymore. Now I must take my leave, but Flora stay strong it will not be for long I promise, goodbye until we meet again.'

Is this real or am I dreaming? I stand watching the road long after Thomas is out of sight, then the sound of Gertie screaming brings me back to earth with a sickening jolt.

`Gertie what is it? Whatever is the matter?' I ask.

Through her sobs she is telling me what has happened, when I see Silas (my father), and Seth (Meg's father) running away from our shed towards Meg's house. When they have gone Gertie and I make our way to the shed to find Jasper lying unconscious but breathing face down just outside the shed.

`Gertie what exactly did you say you were doing?'

`We were climbing up onto the roof like we always do; Jasper lifted me up first, then started to climb up himself. Father saw us, shouting to "get down now" he ran over to the shed. Jasper jumped and fell, I screamed. Seth lifted me down telling me to come and find you, then he said that they would go and get help.'

`Don't start crying again Gertie, go and get me a bowl of water, a towel and some clean rags now, taking care not to fall over yourself.'

What am I going to do? I can't lose my brother; he must not be allowed to die. Before Gertie can return from the house Meg and Hattie are by my side. For the first time in weeks I am able to give way to my true feelings. While I sob freely wrapped securely in Meg's embrace, Hattie begins to attend to Jasper, after only a few minutes, my brother starts moaning and very soon complaining about having his face washed. He was going to be alright, the relief was felt by us all. By the time Gertie got back the situation was much improved. With help Jasper and the rest of us all headed back to our house.

This was certainly a day that I would not forget quickly. First the visit from Thomas, then the drama at the shed with Jasper and Gertie, with the welcome arrival of Hattie and Meg, now strangest of all my father was telling me I didn't have act as lookout tonight. I dare not ask why for fear of a beating, but I am glad for the night off as I will spend it teaching Gertie to read, without father's knowledge of course. Jasper is safely tucked up in bed resting, but the only real damage done was to his pride.

***

Three weeks have passed since Thomas's visit, and this morning I have received a letter telling me that I am to be ready to leave here for good just one week from tomorrow. This has all happened so fast, Jasper and Gertie don't want me to go what am I to do? This is the only chance any of us have got to escape this life for a better one. I must try to speak with Meg and Hattie; they are the only people I can talk to about anything.

I wasn't expecting Meg to be pleased that I was leaving, but Hattie seemed to know all about it already. She has told me to grasp every opportunity I am offered, I just hope Meg will forgive me and that we will remain friends. Hattie is going to keep an eye on Jasper and Gertie until they can join me. So it is all arranged, I am to be collected in a carriage assuming my new identity immediately, only Thomas, his parents, Meg and Hattie will know my new name. Jasper and Gertie are not to be told because they might tell father and he is not to know where I am. Liking the idea of secrets, they think it is exciting to communicate through Meg and Hattie. They are also unaware that they are to join me in the future, but will be sent for when the time is right. This must be kept from them for their own protection.

***

My new life is beginning today, I am now known as Miss Isabella. The horse-drawn carriage continues to rattle towards its destination along the narrow tree-lined lane. I sit on board with no knowledge of what awaits me on my arrival at the Manor. The journey is enjoyable though; the sun is shining giving warmth to the early autumn air.

As the carriage turns yet another corner I finally see what is to be my new home. Fear grips me now as I look towards the enormous house, getting closer and closer.

`I am so glad the weather is nice` I say

to myself,' if it were raining it would look so stark.'

The carriage begins to slow down, I feel myself tighten all over. The carriage draws to a halt; the footman gets down from the front and opens the carriage door.

`Here we are Miss' the footman says, as he holds out his hand to help me down on to the gravel driveway. While my luggage is unloaded, the door opens revealing a well-dressed but not unkindly-looking couple.

`You must be Miss Isabella,' the gentleman remarks before going on to introduce himself, and the elegant lady at his side, `I am Lord Sebastian Havergal, this is my wife Lady Phoebe Havergal, we are so happy that you have agreed to come and live with us.'

`I am most grateful to you Sir; it has been a horrible time for me since...' I break off sobbing. With a comforting arm around my shoulders Lady Phoebe guides me into the house, deciding to talk things through with me after a short time has elapsed, when I have settled in.

The servants at the Manor have been hustling and bustling about making ready for me all day. The master and mistress inform me, they have issued their instructions, determined that everything will be right for me on my arrival.

Not everyone at the house is busy though, in one of the upstairs rooms there is another young girl, Miss Amelia. She is sitting on a window seat in a large bay window, looking wistfully towards the horizon. Small in stature, she has a pale complexion, bright blue eyes, and long golden curls which cascade enchantingly down her back. She can't understand what all the fuss is about. I am just another girl who is coming to live with them, I'm certainly no-one special.

Amelia seems glad that I might be a companion for her, but I also feel as if my presence here has unsettled her, leaving her feeling vulnerable and unsure of her own position. It was Amelia's choice to wait to meet me until lunch-time, but she viewed my arrival with interest from her position in the bay window, above the front door.

My mother never spoke much about her childhood, other than to tell me that her father was a good man, and that both he and her mother were very loving towards her. I knew that her father died when she was a child and that her mother did not live many years afterwards. My mother's life was hard after her father died, so she never wanted to speak about it. This is because she didn't want us children to grow up with any resentment or hatred of anybody, including my father. I only ever met my father's family once, it had been an uneasy meeting, but it was they who decided that they wanted nothing more to do with us or my father. This made my father resentful and angry, which is when the beatings started. I often think he had been hurt by this, although I am greatly afraid of my father, I cannot help but pity him. This only made me want to please him more, but the harder I tried the worse things between us seemed to become. Then after mother had died things became worse than ever, and continued to deteriorate until I left.

***

My mother's letter changed everything, now three weeks into my new life, I am desperate to know what happened between my great-uncle, my mother and grandmother but feel I should not ask as I do not want to open wounds for Lord Sebastian and Lady Phoebe as they have shown me such kindness, welcoming me so warmly into their family home. When I try to ask Thomas he says that I will be told when the time is right. Miss Amelia knows no more of our family history than I do, in fact she doesn't seem to know as much, I am beginning to wonder whether she fits in to the family at all. So I am trying to be patient, but in my heart I know I have to try and find out somehow.

Lady Phoebe is very easy to talk to; I have really been able to begin grieving for my mother and my sister Nettie who died two years earlier since my arrival here. I am already feeling stronger and this afternoon I will be able to speak with her again. Maybe I can even try asking her some questions, without being to searching.

My reading and writing are improving so much since I have been learning properly with a tutor by the name of Miss Grace. It is she who is encouraging me to write poetry as a way of expressing my feelings, releasing the hurts of my past. This activity I really enjoy, finding it both helpful and healing, I have found a real freedom in it. Although I am now called Miss Isabella, I choose to write as Flora Mercy, this is allowed, and what Miss Grace refers to as a `pen name`. I find it quite exciting to have two names, it means that I can close the lid on my old life when the memories are too painful to face.

Jasper and Gertie should be joining me before Christmas, but father is angry that I am no longer there to work for him and keep house. He is trying to stop the younger ones from coming; he wants me back home too. I am beginning to feel the familiar gripping fear once more. Lord Sebastian has promised me that I am safe, so are Jasper and Gertie, but there is an uneasy feeling, a sense of dread that just will not go away. Although father doesn't officially know my whereabouts I can't help feeling that I am being watched. This feeling has been getting stronger since the letter from Meg arrived a week ago, saying how much she is missing me, and would do anything to see me again. Meg also said that my father has changed, being much nicer to her now, and that if I came home, she was certain things would be different. I have never known Meg to lie but there is something about the tone of the whole letter that is making me feel really uncomfortable, I just can't believe what the letter is telling me.

***

It is now late November with the weather unmistakingly beginning to close in. The plans have been made for Jasper and Gertie to join me, but the feeling of being watched is now so strong especially at night, I am crying myself to asleep again.

In front of the mirror in my small attic room, I brush out my long black hair, my green eyes shine with a sense of fulfilment and hope that I have never experienced before. My new life is working out well. I sit still gazing into the mirror, braiding my hair loosely before going to bed, when something or someone appears behind me in the room. I turn to see what is happening but it disappears. Turning back to the mirror it is again clearly visible. Uncertainty is creeping in to my thoughts, my fear turning to terror. I watch this image until I cannot stay awake, is this house beginning to unveil secrets of its own? Or am I right, someone really is watching me?

The image that appeared behind me in the room a week ago has not re-appeared, and my terror is subsiding slightly, becoming more like an uneasiness now, rather than terror. The mystery seems to be deepening however, as I am now hearing noises in the hallway outside my room. I try telling myself that it is just the servants finishing their duties before going to bed themselves, but last night it continued until early this morning. I mentioned this to Thomas at breakfast; he has assured me that he will personally check my room and hallway tonight, to ensure my safety allowing me to sleep without fear. With this knowledge I hope my mind will begin to settle slightly. The noises in the hallway have stopped at the moment, but I still feel as if I am being watched.

***

Today is the first of December with Jasper and Gertie expected in less than a week, my excitement is growing. This is of course dependent on the weather which has started to get much worse in recent days, the journey is too dangerous to undertake in thick snow. A delay in their arrival would be upsetting for me, as it would mean they couldn't join me until the weather improved again in the spring. To be apart for Christmas will be very hard knowing that I now have so much and they still have so little. But, Thomas assures me that if they are unable to join me until the spring their needs will be well provided for, as Lord Sebastian has sent financial support to enable this to happen, and made arrangements with Meg's mother. The thought of being apart for the first Christmas since Mother died also hurts, it is going to be hard, I just wanted us to be together so we are able to support each other through this time.

***

I barely recognize myself these days, the face I see when gazing in the mirror is my own, but instead of looking wild and unkempt my appearance is now that of a lady. Beautifully clothed with my unruly jet-black curls neatly arranged, I feel like a princess in a fairy tale. My life has changed so radically I feel a freedom I have never known before. I sit staring at my reflection, hoping to see something familiar, something I can cling to that will remind me of my mother. But time passes and my memories of her and the life I knew with her are fading.

Mother I miss you so deeply,
I just long to feel your touch,
Why did you leave me so early?

When you knew I loved you so much!

Sometimes I think I can hear you,
Or even see you sat at my side,
Why did you leave me so early?
When you knew I loved you so much!

I know you were ill and so tired,
And no longer had strength to fight,
But why did you leave me so early?
When you knew I loved you so much!

I pray that you are at rest now,
Free from all suffering and pain,
I don't blame you for leaving me early,
And I still love you just as much!

Thank you for being my mother,
And teaching what life should be,
I don't blame you for leaving me early,
And I still love you just as much!

Unfortunately the memories of my father are still as vivid as the day I came; in fact sometimes they are so real that I fear he is really here. I know this is silly, how can he be? I am miles away with a new identity now, but the feeling of being watched, followed, and even pursued is so strong I am in fear of my life again.

A presence so strong I can feel it,
I am almost unable to breathe,
Why can't you just let me be?
Why can't I just break free?
I have left my old life behind me,
A life full of evils and fear,
Please let me embrace my one chance,
Of a life full of love and hope,
The kindness I have been shown,
By people whom I never knew,
Has given me the new start I craved for,
Just forget you ever had me.

Lying here tonight, I cannot sleep, the uneasy feeling that had eased, has come back so strongly I can barely breathe. It is like a suffocating presence that won't go away.

    `Flora, Flora.'

My whole body tightens with fear; I pull the bed clothes tighter around me trying to ignore this voice coming from outside my door.

    `Flora, Flora.'

I can't ignore it anymore!

    `Who are you? Why can't you leave me alone?'

There is a strange yet distant recognition of her voice in my memory, but I am unable to put a name to it.

    `Flora, Flora.'

Why is she calling me by my former name, this is making me even more uncomfortable.

`I am no longer known by that name, I am trying to make a new life and leave the old one behind me. I am now called Miss Isabella, please just go away and leave me to sleep in peace.'

My fear is giving way to terror; I can feel tears' pricking my eyes ready to burst out, my heart is pounding so hard I feel as if I am going to pass out.

`Flora, Flora, I must talk to you, don't you recognise my voice? Can't you guess who I am?'

The recognition in my memory is growing, but I struggle to believe what I am thinking.

`I don't know, should I?'

My mouth is now so dry that my voice betrays my true feelings, more and more each time I speak. Why has nobody else heard what is going on?

`Don't you recognise your only true friend Flora?'

The tears are no longer pricking my eyes, but falling freely from them as I realise whose voice is outside my room. Fear and relief mixed up together are making me dizzy, what is happening?

`Please stop calling me Flora, my name is Miss Isabella, Meg if that is you, why do you have to keep coming at night? How did you get here? Where are you hiding out during the day?'

I need answers but I am scared to know what they will be, and the desperation in Meg's voice is matching the panic in my own she must be terrified too being so far from home, and unlike me she is completely alone here.

`At last fl..., err I mean Miss Isabella, I will explain everything but you must come out into the hallway and then follow me to where we can talk in safety.'

With the knowledge that I am safe in my own room, uncertain of Meg's motives or her safety, I suggest an alternative scenario, unsure what her reaction will be.

`I am not supposed to leave my room at night, so it would be better for you to come in here. No-one would know, and if we are quiet we won't be heard.'

Minutes pass with no response from Meg. The continued silence just increases the anxiety and fear I am already feeling. This entire set of circumstances is so bizarre and unsettling; I decide the silence must be broken.

`Meg are you still there? Are you alright?'

`Yes I am still here, but I am unsure whether your room is the most secure place for us to talk.'

I can sense an unwillingness to even consider my offer coupled with almost an eagerness to take me away from the safety I have while locked in my room. I am beginning to feel as if I am being lured away.

`Well it is certainly safer than whispering through keyholes or creeping along corridors passing other rooms where people are sleeping. If they should wake up and catch us it would take a lot of explaining.' I know this is unlikely but I need to know whether Meg is alone and can be trusted. It is also vital that she trusts me as I get the feeling that her safety is only guaranteed if she successfully leads me into what I am now convinced is a trap set by Silas, probably with the assistance of Seth. Will they stop at nothing to rob me of my new life?

`I suppose you are right, will you please let me in, then we can talk. I can't wait to see you, it has been so long and letters just aren't the same.'
With my heart continuing to pound, tears still falling freely from my eyes, I creep out of bed, across the floor towards the door. Before I turn the key, I take a long pause to steady myself uncertain of the possible danger that may be on the other side.

`Meg, are you alone?'
Waiting for her to respond, I try to peer through the keyhole, but it is too dark to see anything.

`Of course I am!'
The hurt in her voice at my lack of trust is

evident, but there is also a touch of frustration, almost annoyance at my delay in admitting her to my room, which is not like my friend at all. Very gingerly, with my hands trembling I turn the key and open the door.

`Come in quickly! It is good to see you, but you must explain your presence here, tell me everything, I know you well enough to know when you are holding something back.'
I am relieved to see that she is alone, but waste no time in locking the door again once Meg is inside. I can see already that Meg is uneasy with this situation and I sense even more strongly now that she is here under duress.

`Meg, what are you afraid of? Are you in danger? Who is behind all this?'
My friend who has always been so confident and outgoing is now sitting on the floor of my room trembling from head to foot, hugging her knees so tightly and rocking backwards and forwards that I barely recognize her.

`If I give you the answers you want, I will be beaten, if you really care for me you will return with me tonight. I have been sent to bring you home Flora.'
These words are the very words I have been dreading, her unwillingness to use my new name is now the least of my concerns. The mere thought of returning to my old life sends

what feels like shards of ice pulsing through my veins.

`Meg, I can't do that. Even if I could we certainly shouldn't travel that distance at night in this weather. How did you make that journey? The roads are impassable! This opportunity is the only chance Gertie, Ned and I have of a better life, you cannot expect me to give this hope up.'

The terror in Meg's dark brown eyes is obvious, she is hiding things from me, but she is also in need of protection. How can I help her without putting myself in grave danger?

`I didn't come on the roads Flora, but you can only know how I got here if you agree to return home with me.'

I know that I should not agree to this, but the idea of an alternative route which would allow Gertie and Ned to join me for Christmas is so appealing. I feel as though I am being torn apart, if I think rationally, and wish to remain safe, I know I should stay where I am, but if there is even the remotest hope of rescuing my brother and sister, surely I should grab the chance. But I could also put them and me in a situation that is impossible to escape from. My friend's safety, maybe even her life could hang on my decision. What can I do? What will the consequences of my decision be if I opt to stay in safety? I need to talk the whole thing through with

32

someone else, but who? How will they react to the news that someone has managed to find my whereabouts and gain access to the house without being detected? Deciding I can do nothing at this hour of the morning, I try to delay Meg's departure until daylight appears.

`You must be tired and chilled to the bone, please stay here until dawn breaks so that we will at least have daylight on our side.'

Meg immediately jumps up and runs to the door. She is grappling with the key like an animal trying to escape its captors.

`I can't stay any longer, I must leave before dawn. If you don't come now there may not be another chance, please help me Flora.'

`Meg, calm down, I am trying to help you, but returning to my old life is not the answer, you must see that. Please don't make this any harder for me.'

Unable to hide my emotions, I realise I have made my decision; I am staying here where I have felt safe for the first time in years. However, watching my friend in such turmoil is breaking my heart. How can I help Meg if she won't allow me to try?

`Stay here if you must Flora, but let me go now or we may never see each other again.'

Her anguish is so great, that I know I must let

her go. I turn the key to unlock the door, but before opening it, I grab Meg and we hug each other so tightly that it feels as if we will never let go!

`I love you like a sister you know that I always have, but I must respect my mother's dying wish Meg, please try and understand.'
Meg smiles weakly at me but without another word, scampers away so fast into the darkness of the hallway so that before I can get through the door myself she has vanished in an unknown direction. I close the door and return to my bed, although I know that any further sleep is highly unlikely.

Lying here in the dark, with the knowledge that I am safe and secure in my room, I cannot get Meg out of my head. She was afraid, leading me to believe she was in danger and I can't think how I can help. If I had gone with her both our lives could have been in jeopardy, but by choosing to stay and obeying my mother's dying wish, have I abandoned my friend to a fate I dare not contemplate? With an overwhelming feeling of guilt and foreboding I again begin to sob into my pillow, when a chilling draught interrupts my anguished reverie. Where is it coming from? Getting out of bed to check my door which I know I locked, my heart is again starting to pound. My growing sense of dread is causing me to fight to keep my breathing under control which is making me feel quite dizzy. A timid voice breaks the stifling silence.

`Miss Isabella, look in your mirror.'

The sound of that voice sends shivers down my spine.

`Why? Miss Amelia you are scaring me. How did you get in here? What do you want?'

My door is locked as I knew it would be, so what is going on?

`Miss Isabella, please look in the mirror. One of the answers you seek will be revealed if you do!'

Trembling all over I turn to look in the mirror. To my amazement, although with a certain amount of relief, Miss Amelia is standing in a narrow unlit doorway in the wall opposite my mirror, at right angles to my door.

`Have you been here before Miss Amelia?'

`I have, it was me you caught sight of before but I was too shy to speak and I needed to know you better before I let you in on this secret. This doorway links our two rooms by a narrow unlit passage, and I hoped we could use it to see each other privately. Do you think we can?'

Feeling slightly relieved and strangely comforted by this news, I see an escape route from the danger and terror of my own room.

`I would like that, thank you. I would

love to know you better and be friends.'
 ` I'd like that too.'
A sudden sense of reality hits me, my fear intensifying rapidly, what is happening here? Why is Miss Amelia standing in my room in the dark hours of early morning talking about a secret?

 `Miss Amelia, what secret are you talking about? Is it this secret doorway and passage you have already told me about, or is there something else?'
The tremble in my voice betraying my feelings. Closing the door behind her and walking towards me she begins to tell me her story.

Amelia and I did not part company until dawn was breaking and the first shards of light were breaking through the heavy velvet blackness of the enormous countryside sky. Leaving quickly by the secret passage she is silent as neither her nor I want to be discovered and have to explain this situation. This morning I am desperate that my lack of sleep is not obvious to anyone, as no-one can know about my night-time visitors. Miss Amelia did not even know that she was the second. This secrecy is vital as Meg is very much in my mind, and her very life could be in jeopardy should the wrong person or people ever discover her visit, or worse still her whereabouts and the route she travelled to get here.

Miss Amelia's story last night has convinced me of what I had suspected for some time. She has also been rescued from a life of fear and poverty; I hope that this will bring us closer together as we get to know each other better. One thing that she said though has left me feeling uneasy, leading me to believe that our lives may be more closely linked than either of us realise. We are the same age and both have two younger siblings, Miss Amelia's sister Lottie is the same age as Jasper, her brother Jesse the same age as Gertie. They too are supposed to be joining their sister in a new life here, but again the weather has made this impossible at this time. I also discovered that she only arrived a month before me, which explains her timidity and reluctance to meet me the day of my arrival. At the moment we are learning our lessons with Miss Grace at separate times, but we both want to ask if we can learn together so that our friendship can grow. Miss Amelia uses drawing and painting as an outlet for her emotions, in the same way that I use my poetry. Drawing and painting both interest me but poetry is my first love at this time.

***

I am enjoying my new found friendship with Miss Amelia, but the more time that passes, the more fearful for Meg's safety I become. Two weeks have elapsed since that night; the weather continues to get worse. The weather could be to blame, but there has been no letter from her and she has not paid me another visit either. A sense of dread is building inside me, my greatest fear being that there is nothing I can do to help her. Should I have gone with her that night? Have I cost my friend her life?

I now know that I have to speak to Lady Phoebe about the great wrong which my mother suffered in childhood as soon as possible. I can't get rid of the feeling that there is something linking my family to Miss Amelia's, and I must know what it is. This afternoon Lady Phoebe has asked to speak with me, so I hope I might finally discover the truth about my mother. The link between myself and Miss Amelia might also be made known to me. I knock on the door of Lady Phoebe's sitting room as I always do, expecting the usual pause before being asked to enter. Today, to my surprise, Lady Phoebe opens the door to me herself, ushering me to the large window seat overlooking the beautiful gardens below, which lay sleeping under a blanket of pure white snow.

`My dear I need to tell you something this afternoon which I hope will help you understand why we wanted so much to help you. Please listen to what I have to say very carefully, allowing me to finish before asking any questions, is this alright?'

Relieved to finally be hearing the story I've been longing to know since my arrival here, hoping for some answers, but also feeling anxious about what is to come. The distinct tremble in my voice giving away my feelings.

`Yes Lady Phoebe, I need to know what happened.'

Sitting beside me with her hands grasping my own to reassure me she begins to explain the story which is so important to me, and which I need to know.

`My husband, Lord Sebastian, is your mother's cousin. His father was your mother's uncle, and your grandfather's younger brother. Your grandfather being the eldest son naturally had the right to live in and inherit the family home, along with his wife and new baby daughter. That baby was your mother, Martha. His brother was very jealous of this, but knew it was your grandfather's birthright and nothing could be done to change things. He too was well provided for, but nothing was ever good enough for him. Then a tragedy occurred. Your mother was only eight years old when her father died, and your grandmother had no legal rights to the property, as it was owned by her husband's family. Unfortunately, your mother's grandparents had already died, so the estate immediately became the property of dear Martha's uncle. He was a cruel man and resented anyone who was not his blood relation, he also considered any female children to be worthless. Your mother and grandmother were ordered to leave the estate immediately with nothing other than a tiny inheritance which your grandmother's father had left her. This did not last long, and very soon Martha and her mother had to find work to survive.'

The feeling of tears and anger welling up inside me is almost too much to bear, seeing my anguished torment Lady Phoebe puts her arm around me pulling me close before continuing.

`As an only child, Martha had received a high standard of education until her father died, but when forced to leave her childhood home somehow managed to keep the few books her father had been able to provide for her. Worse was to follow when eventually a local family took your grandmother and mother in, they were forced to work as servants in return for food and lodging. Your mother's childhood soon became one of drudgery and bullying. The son of the household, Silas, later to become your father, was ten years older than your mother, and when she turned sixteen she was forced to marry him in payment for the so called kindness shown to her and her mother. Your grandmother had sadly died five years earlier, leaving an eleven year old Martha completely alone. Your sister Nettie was born shortly after they were married and the three of them remained with your father's family until your mother became pregnant again. When you were born and were another girl your parents were given enough money to buy a small house, on the condition that it was away from your father's family. The reason for this harsh treatment was because two girls brought no hope of a proper heir to inherit the estate so you were not wanted, and any further association with you was considered worthless. Most of the rest you know, apart from how we knew what was happening. As children Martha and Sebastian were very close, and as Sebastian was older than Martha he was determined to protect her. When your mother was sent away by his father, Sebastian was angry and knew he had to try and keep an eye on her. This he did, first with the help of his mother who was against what her husband had done, but had no authority or courage to prevent it. Later direct letters were sent secretly between Martha and Sebastian. So when your mother's final letter arrived he was heartbroken, but knew he could finally start putting right the great wrong which had taken place all those years ago by helping you to have a better life. Now my child do you understand? '

Sobbing and trembling I nod my head, as words will not come at this time. Now I know why my mother never talked about her childhood, it was too painful for her and she wanted to protect me from the hurts which she had suffered. Trying hard to compose myself, I know I need the answers to two questions, so still trembling I ask the first one.

`Please Lady Phoebe, if my father's family wanted nothing to do with us, why did they come to visit us once? '

Looking at me Lady Phoebe seems surprised that I even remember that day, as I was so young.

`How old were you when they came?'

I knew that Jasper was only just four so that means I must have been seven.

`I think I was seven, but the only person they seemed interested in was Jasper, and they didn't even want to see the rest of us. I can remember that they would only speak to my father, my mother being dismissed as though she didn't matter.'

`Yes child that was the reason for their visit, they knew when your brother had been born that they finally had a male heir for the estate, but they decided that they would only visit when he would be old enough to return to the estate with them so that he could be educated appropriately. Your mother was distraught when the plan of their visit was made clear to her, and Martha begged Silas to stop them from taking her son. He then surprised everyone, especially his parents, by saying that he had no intention of letting his son go to be brought up by people who were not prepared to support the only son they had given birth too. Silas also knew he needed a boy to learn his trade. This made your father's parents furious and that was why they never retuned and severed all contact. You are well aware though that nature dealt a cruel blow and your brother has very poor eyesight so he became useless to your father, in fact Silas saw him as a burden, but knew he had to protect him as the only male child. It was after this that first your poor sister Nettie, then after her tragic death, you were made to be useful to him. Dearest Martha hated what was happening but was powerless to change or prevent any of it. That is why we had to bring you here under our protection and as soon as the weather breaks, Jasper and Gertie will join you here as part of our family.'

Never knowing that poor Nettie had been used as I had by our father, another question needs to be answered.

`Lady Phoebe, please will you tell me why Nettie died?'

The tears are again falling from my eyes and

the words catch in my throat.

`Dear child this is a lot for you to bear, are you sure you want to continue now?'

`I must, I need to know before I can really be me, and live the life my mother wanted me too.'

`You are brave and loyal, and obviously just as devoted to your mother, as Martha was to hers. Your sister was acting as a lookout for your father just as you did, but slipped one night and fell off the cliff. It was this tragedy that was the initial cause of your mother's illness. She never could forgive Silas for putting Nettie in that perilous location. Martha never came to terms losing her daughter in that horrific way, so when Silas began using you for the same purpose she was desperate that you should be protected. That was the message which was contained in her final letter to Sebastian.'

Stunned and fearful I try to absorb what I have just discovered, maybe now would be a good time to tell Lady Phoebe about my visits from Meg and Amelia two weeks ago. I am now so afraid that some dreadful fate has befallen Meg, I am frantic with concern and really don't know whether my explaining any of it will help her or me. Then turning to me Lady Phoebe's expression changes from one of mild concern to one of real anxious worry.

`My sweet child, something is

troubling you please let me in to your secret, I may be able to help.'

Now was my chance I must do something to try and help Meg, and I must know what links me to Miss Amelia.

`Lady Phoebe, two weeks ago in the middle of the night, I was woken by a voice outside my room. I was frightened but I tried to ignore it, knowing my door was locked, I knew I was safe. When I didn't answer I hoped that the voice would just stop, but it called me again, using my old name, causing me to become more and more afraid.'

Just talking about that night and having to relive it, I could feel the same pounding in my chest and breathless panic, which I had felt in my room two weeks earlier.

`Eventually I knew I had to respond, so I told the voice that I no longer used that name and to please leave me alone. The strangest part of all this was that somewhere in my memory I knew this voice. The strangely familiar voice was persistent and sounded almost as terrified as I felt. Then in an instant that sent a chill right through me, I realized who I was talking too, it didn't make sense. How could Meg be here? She wanted me to go somewhere with her so we could talk, knowing this would not be safe for either of us, and suspecting a trap set by my father; I managed to persuade her to come in to my room. I only opened my door after Meg had convinced me that she was alone. We talked for a long time but the answers I'd hoped for never came. Then when I suggested she stayed until dawn broke so that daylight would be there to make travel safer, Meg jumped up and flew to the door desperate to get out. I had to let her go, but ever since that night I have had a feeling of dread that Meg's life is as much at risk as my own. Our conversation also led me to fear that this was the case. I couldn't go with her, but since that night, I have been left wondering whether I have cost my friend her life. How could she have got here through the severe winter weather? How can I help her? I have heard nothing from her since, please help me!'

I can talk no more; I am exhausted and sobbing emphatically. Lady Phoebe is holding me close to her, trying to console me, but I can sense a difference in her too. When after a long time I look again into her kind face, she is looking deeply troubled.

`Isabella, I hoped that you were safe here, but it appears that Silas has re-opened the underground tunnels, and managed to persuade your friend to try and take you back with her. You are right to be anxious for Meg; she may very well be in danger. I need to speak with Lord Sebastian, but with what you have now told me it may not be possible for

Jasper and Gertie to join you here after all. You may not be able to stay either, but don't fret my child, you will certainly never return to the life you left behind.'

This latest revelation cuts through me like an arrow, I begin to fear that I may never see my brother and sister again.

`Will Jasper and Gertie be alright?' I ask, but the words hardly come out.

`They are not at risk like you are, and you are all safer if they stay where they are. We hoped it wouldn't come to this but all links with your old home and life may have to be severed completely.'

Now I must find the link between Miss Amelia and myself. If I am to lose my own siblings I must have someone to share my life with, but I can't ask now, I feel numb and bereft of hope again. What does my future hold now? Is my life to be turned upside down again?

I sit and stare out of the window, not hearing or feeling anything. Lady Phoebe has asked Miss Grace to sit with me while she talks to Lord Sebastian about what has happened, and what can be done to ensure my continued safety.

The last threads of light have all but disappeared from the ever darkening sky before Lady Phoebe returns. So gently she takes my hand before saying anything.

`Isabella, Lord Sebastian and I both feel you are safe to stay here for the moment, but the underground tunnel network must be shut down. This cannot be done until after Christmas, so you are to share Miss Amelia's room until the work can be done.'

Unsure about how this will help, and worried about the secret passage linking the two rooms, I know I have to explain my other visit that took place on the same night as Meg's. Lady Phoebe did not seem surprised when I told her, and assured me that the passage could only be accessed from those two rooms, and that it could still provide a way of escape or a hiding place if ever this became necessary. She also told me that Miss Amelia is the daughter of Lord Sebastian's brother. Her mother died in child birth so Amelia never knew her mother. When her father married again and her step-mother gave birth to two children of her own, because she had always resented Amelia she treated her like a servant making her care for the younger children, and she beat her regularly. This means we are distant cousins, and knowing this gave me a small glimmer of hope back. We could finally start building a real friendship.

With a jolt my mind again went to Meg's plight, and how my father had discovered my location. I also couldn't work out how he would know about an underground tunnel network leading to a property which he had never been to, panic is again gripping my very being.

`Lady Phoebe, can anything be done to help Meg?'

There is a long pause before she hesitantly responds.

`I don't know yet, it might already be too late, but rest assured that everything that can be done will be done. I won't make promises which can't be kept. My best advice to you is to pray for her alright child?'

I nod my head knowing the only outlet for my anguish is to write a poem for her, which will allow me to cling to the hope that she may soon be rescued. Someday I can give it or send it to her when we are both safe and the dark threat that overshadows both our lives has ended.

Lady Phoebe tells me that the network of underground tunnels has always been well known among smugglers, but how my father discovered that I am living here, is of grave concern to both herself and Lord Sebastian. There are only two possible explanations, either Meg or her mother were beaten until Silas and Seth discovered what they wanted to know, or someone from within Lord Sebastian's household has been acting on my father's behalf, using the tunnels to pass information to him or a third person, possibly Meg. If the second option is true then I could be in more danger than I have ever been before.

Today has been exhausting, but having joined Miss Amelia in her room, the knowledge that I am not alone is giving me a little comfort and reassurance. I fear sleep will not come easily tonight though as my life is again in turmoil, the uncertainty surrounding Meg's whereabouts and safety as well as not knowing where my father may be hiding is filling me with dread. Will Silas come himself to try and take me back? Will Meg come again? Part of me is hoping she will, so at least I would know she is still alive. But another part hopes that she stays away, because it will mean we are both still in grave danger. Is Miss Amelia now at risk as well? Is my presence in her room a threat to her safety? When will this torment ever end?

***

This morning I awake to find more snow has fallen over night, and is continuing to fall. I managed to sleep after all, being so tired my eyes just would not stay open, despite the terror and anguish I was feeling. Miss Amelia is already up and dressed, but as yet has not gone down for breakfast. In fact she is standing at our door appearing to be listening for something, or someone. I get up out of bed, but before I can even join her at the bedroom door, she tells me to be quiet. The sound of men's voices shouting reaches my ears before I get to the door. My blood turns to ice in my veins, one of those voices belongs to my father, I knew it instantly, the other is the rich kindly voice of Lord Sebastian. The absolute terror shows in my face, and Miss Amelia's concern is evident.

`Miss Isabella, are you alright? You are so pale.'

Unable to speak, I shake my head and run back to the bed where I curl up into a ball with the covers wrapped tightly around me. Barely able to breath, and with tears quickly blurring my vision my head begins to spin, what is going to happen now? I am rigid unable to move or speak for what seems like hours, in reality it is only a few minutes that passes before Miss Amelia crosses the room towards me. However, before she is able to speak the sound of footsteps can be heard approaching our room. They are coming from the secret passage that joins this room to mine, my panic builds, my heart is pounding, but the steps are not heavy enough for fathers. Then the narrow door from the passageway opens and Lady Phoebe appears, but she is not alone. Behind her is Thomas who is carrying something, as he enters the light of the room I can see it is a young girl lying motionless in his arms. I know in an instant that it is Meg. Seeing the look on my face Lady Phoebe takes my hand drawing me towards her.

`Is she alive?'

My question is no more than a whisper, but the answer is one I am desperate for.

`She is, but Meg is gravely ill she was found trying to get into your room, but collapsed soon afterwards. We think she had been living in the tunnels since her last visit to you to avoid your father, but he followed her here so she was trying to escape from him by coming to your room.'

`Has…. has my father gone? I heard him shouting downstairs.'

`He has, and you are now quite safe. Lord Sebastian and your father have come to an agreement. You are to stay here with us, but all contact with Jasper and Gertie must cease immediately.'

`But why, I promised mother that I would look after them and help them escape to a better life.'

`We do not intend to stop helping them, but things will have to be done differently from now on.'

`Is Meg staying with us?'

`She is, at least until she recovers, then it is a decision for her and her mother to make. Now Seth is no longer there she may be needed at home.'

`I don't understand why Seth is no longer there? '

`Seth was caught by the authorities during the last smuggling trip, he is in prison awaiting sentence, unless he names the rest of the gang including your father he will face the gallows. There is a loyalty among smugglers which means that is very unlikely.

Thomas take Meg into Isabella's room and fetch blankets, hot water and clean clothes immediately, we must do for her all we can until the doctor can get here, which looking out there will not be for several days. Isabella get washed and dressed, then you and Miss Amelia must have some breakfast. When you have finished come up to your room and you may sit with Meg for a while, but she needs to rest so you must not try to wake her. I will be at her side with you so don't be afraid.'

I say nothing, but immediately do as Lady Phoebe asks, making sure I have writing materials with me to write Meg's poem.

Meg you were my only friend,
Our childhood was tough,
But the love we shared between us,
Gave me hope when times were rough.
The bond in which we found our strength,
Can never be lost or broken,
Though distance separates us now,

Our friendship is still strong,
The unity we share together,
Will enrich my life forever.

On entering I notice that the curtains are drawn and a roaring fire is burning, casting dancing shadows all around the room. Meg, now dressed in clean clothes, is lying in the bed with thick blankets covering her. Fear starts to grip me once more as I approach Lady Phoebe who is sitting beside the bed.

`Come and sit here with me Isabella, Meg needs to know she has a friend. When she wakes up she will not know where she is, and she must not be allowed to panic or get upset as this will not help her recovery. Seeing your face will reassure her that she is safe.'

Standing at the foot of the bed, not daring to go nearer, seeing my friend so pale and thin brings back painful memories of the last day I saw my mother alive just a few short months earlier.

`I'm frightened, the last time I saw someone like this was…..'

No longer able to talk, my face tells the rest of the story.

`Come, sit with me, this is not the same as your mother child, Meg is tired, yes she is very sick, but with good care and the love of her friend she can recover from this. You have been through so much together, Meg came here to help you, she didn't let you down, so I know you won't let her down either. I will be here with you and we will care for her together. With Christmas just over a week away and Jasper and Gertie not able to be with you, at least you and Meg will have each other. If she is well enough to get up it would be very special for both of you, wouldn't it?'

` Yes it would, but will she get better?' Saying nothing, Lady Phoebe takes my hand and squeezes it gently to comfort me, but the dancing shadows and warm glow from the fire have taken on a far more sinister appearance and comfort feels a long way off at the present time.

***

Today is the twenty-first of December; Meg has been here five days. Her condition has barely changed and she has only opened her eyes twice in this time. She still has a fever and the doctor has only been able to see her once because of the weather. Concern for Meg is growing and I am now dreading Christmas day. I don't want to lose my friend, but I know the more time that passes the chance of her recovering gets less. I hate to see her like this; she should not have to suffer this way.

My eyes are so sore with tiredness and

almost constant crying, I have not been able to sleep properly since Meg's arrival. Lady Phoebe is very concerned that I will be ill myself, but is at a loss as to how best to help me, lessen my heartache or ease my anguish. I sit at my friends' bedside with Lady Phoebe, watching, waiting for some sign of improvement, not really seeing or hearing anything.

`How can I help her, what can I do?'
Lady Phoebe takes my hands, clasping them in hers, before saying the words that I least want to hear.

`Isabella, there is no more we can do, Meg has to fight this herself, and at the moment she is losing that fight. You must never give up hope, but I fear we must be prepared for the worst.'
I can say nothing, but tears are again starting to flow. Lady Phoebe draws me to her, and I curl up with my head in her lap and gently, she strokes my hair, I drift off to sleep even though I try to fight it I can no longer keep my eyes open.

I awaken with a jolt, immediately becoming aware that Lady Phoebe and I have been joined in Meg's room by another person. Opening my eyes and struggling to focus in the dim light I realise that the doctor has again made it through the weather and is tending to Meg. Lady Phoebe continues to gently stroke my hair, I am quite content to stay with my head in her lap, this is the most at ease I have felt for days. There is a stillness and a peace in the room I have not been aware of before, knowing this I relax back into a restful sleep.

I awake this time with a shiver, a noticeable chill has come over the room. Rubbing my eyes and sitting myself up, I can see that the life of my friend has come to an end while I slept. Tears are falling freely again as Lady Phoebe, now standing beside me holds me so tenderly, that although my grief is great for the second time this year at the loss of someone I loved dearly, the strange calm that was in the room earlier returns to me even more strongly. I know how much I will miss my friend who had been like a sister to me, but I also know that she is now safe, and can no longer be beaten and used by men who care only about themselves and their dark trade.

Grief is a hurt that won't subside,
A pain in your heart that you want to hide,
The people you miss,
On the wind, send a kiss,
And you know they have not left your side.

The love that you feel for each other still lives,

And as time goes by hurts will heal,
You will never forget loved ones, who've passed,
And memories last a lifetime.
 The people you miss,
On the wind, send a kiss,
And you know they have not left your side.

Part two

Miss Amelia and I are now eighteen years old and as close as Meg and I had been in childhood. The first Christmas I spent at Havergal Manor was very hard, not least because Meg had died just four days earlier. But my life since then has been extremely good, filled with happiness and joy. Miss Grace, my tutor has been so impressed with my ability to learn, that she has suggested I may like to consider becoming a governess or tutor myself. At first the whole idea of this was quite terrifying, but both Lady Phoebe and Lord Sebastian are extremely encouraging and supportive. I now feel that this may be the new challenge that I need.

I have been shown so much kindness and love since I arrived here three years ago, I would love to be able to give something back. If the best way for me to do this is by providing other children with knowledge and learning, then I will follow this path for my life willingly.

Miss Amelia is to remain at Havergal Manor and does not want me to leave either; I am the only real friend she has ever had. I would love to stay as I am very happy and settled here, but if I am to be a governess then I would be expected to live in. I would still visit the Manor regularly, and Lady Phoebe has told me that she would not want me to be too far away. My father could still be a risk, especially if he discovered that I was no longer living in the care and protection of Lord Sebastian, and both Lord Sebastian and Lady Phoebe want me to feel that I am welcome to return at any time.

Miss Grace, together with Lord Sebastian are already looking into possible appropriate appointments, my application letter is written and ready to send when a position has been found for me. My poetry is still very important to me and Lady Phoebe assures me that this and my love of learning will be of great benefit to me in attaining a position as a governess.

***

Miss Amelia has used her love of art to illustrate some of my poems which now hang in the library. We are both greatly appreciative of all the encouragement we receive daily from Lord Sebastian, Lady Phoebe and Thomas. I still have no direct contact with Jasper and Gertie, father is still smuggling so danger surrounds him constantly. I do know though that Jasper and Gertie are being cared for from a distance by

Lord Sebastian, who still intends that they should have the same chance that I have benefited from. This will happen even if my father has to die first, and with every new smuggling trip undertaken the risks he is taking become greater, making the chances of him being caught evermore likely. Whatever I suffered as a child, Silas is still my father and I pray every night that he will see the error of his ways and accept the help that Lord Sebastian has offered to him.

***

Meg's father refused to reveal any names to the authorities so was hung three years ago; Hattie lost both her daughter and her husband within a week. However, Hattie and her two younger children, Agnes and Ned, now live in a lodge only a few miles away which Lord Sebastian owns. When Meg died he felt he needed to help them in some way, Hattie just cooks twice a week for an elderly lady in return for this hospitality. This suits her very well and Agnes and Ned are visited by Miss Grace once a week, and are now able to read and write as well as Meg used to.

***

Everything is happening at once, my application letter was sent to a family living locally and I am to visit them this very day. My first memory of houses like this is from my very early childhood. They have always filled me with trembling fear, but now, here I am, striding up the driveway towards an enormous front door belonging to one such property. I have applied for the post of governess to the three young girls who live here. I have been granted an interview, so this is my chance to overcome my fear of imposing places, and to show that I am the person they are looking for to educate their children.

As I approach the front door my heart is pounding and my stomach feels as if it is tying itself in knots, what am I doing here? What on earth makes me think I can ever do what is expected of a governess? With a trembling hand, and feeling hot and cold at the same time, I reach for the bell and pull down hard. Hearing the faint, distant ring and knowing it will take a while for it to be answered, my instinct is to turn and run away from this place as fast as I can, but strangely I cannot move, something is keeping me here. This I cannot explain, my panic seems to be increasing and yet a peculiar sense of calm appears to be washing over me, it is as if I know I am needed in this imposing, dark and isolated place. What is happening?

The door is eventually opened by a mature, well-dressed gentleman with a solemn yet not unkindly expression, who beckons me in telling me to take a seat in the drawing room.

I am not kept waiting long, before an elegantly dressed, pleasant looking young woman enters and introduces herself as Lady Elizabeth Benfleet, the lady of the house and mother to the three girls whom I have come to serve if I am given this position.

The interview, which was a very new and daunting experience for me seemed to go well. Lady Elizabeth is charming and the three girls, Mary, Sarah and Harriet are quite delightful. Mary and Sarah are twins aged eight and Harriet is only just six. We seem to form a bond instantly and Lady Elizabeth has promised to notify me of her decision before the end of the week.

Walking back towards Havergal Manor I can't escape the feeling that there is something which I have not been told. When I enquired about Sir Abraham, Lady Elizabeth's husband and the father of the three girls, Lady Elizabeth said that I would meet him in time but the girls' education was her responsibility. She did not seem to want to talk about him at all, and this leaves me feeling rather uneasy. Perhaps Lady Phoebe can explain further as she knows the family and was very happy for me to apply for the position of governess with them.

The walk home is pleasant in the early autumn sunshine and by the time I reach the Manor I feel at ease and happy. Lady Phoebe immediately asks me into the drawing room, wanting to know how I got on. I told her that I would hear by the end of the week, and if successful would be expected to start at the beginning of October. She appears satisfied with this arrangement, but is pleased that I do not have to leave immediately.

`Did you meet Sir Abraham, Isabella?'
I was slightly surprised by this question, but saw this as my chance to get some answers and hopefully put my mind at ease.

`Not on this occasion, I was told that I would meet him in time. Lady Elizabeth told me that any decision regarding the girls' education was down to her. '
Lady Phoebe seemed almost relieved at this piece of news, and got out her needlework.

`That is probably for the best. Did you meet the children?'
Unsure what she meant by her statement my initial uneasiness began to increase.

`Oh yes, the three little girls are quite delightful and they seemed to warm to me instantly. But why is everyone so secretive about Sir Abraham is there something I should be aware of?'
At first Lady phoebe seems reluctant to answer, but then her expression changes again, and carefully putting down her needlework comes over to join me in the window seat.

`Lady Elizabeth and Sir Abraham are very much in love Isabella, it is important you know that before I say more.'

This seems a strange thing to say, but knowing Lady Phoebe as well as I do, there is certainly a very good reason behind it.

`Please carry on; I don't doubt their devotion to each other. The children are so happy.'

`Sir Abraham was married once before, and so is much older than Lady Elizabeth. There is an older daughter from his first marriage who also lives with them but when her mother died she refused to speak, and to my knowledge has not spoken since. Miss Ruth must be fifteen by now, but rarely leaves her room and has never accepted Lady Elizabeth or her younger sisters. Sir Abraham has been so concerned for Miss Ruth for so long now that he too has become withdrawn and rarely leaves the house. You should also know that he was accused of causing his first wife's death, though this was nonsense as she had never been strong and died from influenza when Miss Ruth was only three years old. It was not the authorities who accused him, but his wife's family. So trying to do the best for his young daughter, he decided he ought to marry again and give her a new mother. This was also the only way his first wife's parents would allow Miss Ruth to remain in his care, it took four years before he met and married Lady Elizabeth, who had originally come to Benfleet Hall as a Nanny to Miss Ruth. This was not considered a suitable match but when Miss Ruth's grandparents tried to take her to live with them she refused to go, and since then there has been no contact between them. Sir Abraham has never forgiven himself for the death of his first wife, or as he sees it, for depriving Miss Ruth of a relationship with her maternal grandparents. He finds any new person in the household quite threatening and disruptive; the only person he is able confide anything in is his young nephew Benedict, who is going into the ministry to become Reverend at the church near Benfleet Hall. He is twenty-one and having lost both parents when he was just sixteen is also living at Benfleet Hall. He is very quiet but a charming young man nonetheless and the only one who can get close to Sir Abraham. So you see Isabella, why a governess is needed for the young daughters of Lady Elizabeth.'

These revelations are almost a relief to me as I feared a more sinister background, similar to the one I myself had been rescued from.

`Do you think in time I may be allowed to try and help Miss Ruth Lady Phoebe? I would hate her to be excluded, and because of what I have been through I would like the opportunity to try and help if I can.'

Smiling tenderly and taking my hand, Lady Phoebe's answer is a surprise and a relief.

`I hoped you would say that Isabella, when I spoke with Lady Elizabeth before your interview, I told her some of your story. She was so delighted that finally someone might understand how Miss Ruth felt and what she had been through. She knows the only way to help Sir Abraham is for Miss Ruth to be helped, but Sir Abraham would not accept a governess for Miss Ruth as he feels any further disturbance to her routine may be too much. But he did agree to a governess for the three younger girls. You will have to be patient with Sir Abraham and allow him to get used to you being there first, but I am sure that in time he will allow you to meet Miss Ruth and be a companion to her if nothing else.'

Hearing all this I now know what prevented me from running away this morning, when I stood trembling at the huge front door. I really am needed by this household, and have the opportunity to change someone else's life for the better, just as mine has been changed.

***

Three days have passed since I attended my interview at Benfleet Hall, and this morning a letter has arrived for me. Afraid to open it and of what it might say, I have decided to wait until after lunch when Miss Amelia and I are together for our lessons. As lunchtime approaches I start to question whether I even want to leave Havergal Manor, and both Miss Amelia and Miss Grace have said how much they will miss me. Despite all this I know there is a family at Benfleet Hall that need me, and who I really feel I can help. Lunchtime is here and although I intended to open the letter after lunch, Lady Phoebe and Lord Sebastian also want to know my news. So after we have eaten, I open the small white envelope.

The position of governess at Benfleet Hall to Sarah, Mary and Harriet is mine. I am to arrive at Benfleet Hall in time to take up my duties on the first Monday in October. Lady Phoebe is delighted for me and despite not wanting me to go, so is Miss Amelia. I am after all only a short distance away, and will be able to visit when my duties allow. The time frame I have got to prepare myself is just two weeks, but there is an excitement building inside me now, although I am still feeling anxious as well. This is a huge responsibility for me and I really hope I don't let the family down, or Lady Phoebe. She has given me so much that I am determined to fulfil my duties to the best of my ability so as not to let her down. I owe all this to the love of my mother who quite literally gave her life so that I could escape from a life of drudgery and fear, I cannot help but shed a tear when I think about this and also what it cost my childhood friend to try and keep me safe.

As I bid farewell,
To my haven of safety,
Full of friends,
And people who care,
I step out in faith,
To the challenge ahead,
In the hope I can help,
As I have been helped,
Bringing unity back,
To a family that hurts,
And joy to lives where there is none.

***

Today I am leaving Havergal Manor to take up my post as governess at Benfleet Hall. My emotions are mixed, tears are not far away, but I know that there are friends and people who live close by and my visits here will be very special. Lord Sebastian is insisting on personally escorting me during the short journey to Benfleet Hall, and the carriage ride will be beautiful through the trees displaying their jewel coloured leaves in the autumn sunshine. Not wanting to make things harder for me all the goodbyes were said after lunch. The only person to accompany Lord Sebastian and I to the carriage is Lady Phoebe, who embraces me before I take my seat in the carriage.

`You know where we are and that you are welcome anytime Isabella.'

Not daring to speak I nod and quickly get up into the carriage. As we pull away and start down the driveway I wave but dare not look back, tears are already falling. Knowing I cannot arrive at my new home and employers crying, I quickly try to compose myself by concentrating on the inspiring autumn scene that I am travelling through.

The journey is over almost too quickly and as we slow to a stop outside the Hall, a face at a window holds my gaze. It is a young girl whose expression is so sad; I know at once that it must be Miss Ruth. When she realises that I have seen her though she immediately disappears from view and the curtains are drawn. I alight from the carriage still reflecting on this image when the huge front door is opened and Lady Elizabeth comes out to greet me.

`Welcome, Miss Isabella please come in and make your way to the drawing room where we will take tea together before Lord Sebastian leaves. You will join us Sebastian?'

`I would be delighted Elizabeth, thank you for the invitation.'

The three of us took tea and Lord Sebastian left before the light of day had faded. Sir Abraham did not join us but did come and meet me before Lady Elizabeth took me up to my room. My heart went out to this very gentle, sensitive man weighed down with guilt and concern. Positioned at the back of the house overlooking the prettiest garden I have ever seen my room is charming. Light streams in through the large bay window, and there is a small window seat which thrills me. I am delighted with my room and spend the rest of the afternoon planning out lessons for the following day. Miss Grace was kind enough to give me some old lesson plans to use a guide, but planning is a learning experience for me which at the present time is very daunting. This is only possible because my luggage had already been brought up and unpacked.

***

Returning to my room after dinner tonight is the first time I begin to feel alone and slightly fearful. I have no escape route from here and my mind begins to turn to thoughts of my father. Will he find out where I am, now that I have left the safety of Havergal Manor? Will he try again to force me to return to a life which I now have barely any recognition of? Then it hits me like fork lightening, if there were tunnels leading to

Havergal Manor, could there also be a network leading to Benfleet Hall? Sleep now feels a long way off, but knowing the responsibility I have to undertake tomorrow, I force myself to close my eyes and try to put fearful thoughts out of my head. Initially I toss and turn, jumping at the slightest sound, but eventually tell myself that there is no-one who knows I am here, apart from people I really trust and love dearly back at Havergal Manor, none of whom would ever betray me.

***

This morning I was woken with a gentle tap on my door by a maid with my morning tea tray. This is not something I have been used to, but it is most welcome after a very restless night. I wash, dress and make my way downstairs to breakfast. Lady Elizabeth is already there, beckoning to me to take a seat next to her; the girls are also already seated and eating.

`Did you sleep well Miss Isabella?'
Not wanting to appear ill at ease on my first day, I explain only that once I get used to my new surroundings I am sure I will sleep very well.

`My room is delightful Lady Elizabeth and the bed very comfortable. I shall settle in quickly I am sure, and am very grateful for you providing me with such an opportunity.'

`You are most welcome, if there is

anything you need, want to know, or we can do to make you more comfortable, please just ask and I will ensure it is fulfilled.'

`Thank you, but I am more than happy and you have already made me most welcome.'

After breakfast I return to my room and collect the lesson plans for today, taking them with me to the school room. The girls are expected a ten o'clock to commence their lessons, so I have enough time to sit and prepare myself for my first day as tutor rather than student. Arriving at the school room I discover that the door is already open, but when I enter the room appears to be empty. I begin setting out my lesson plans and ensure that each child has the materials they will need this morning. The school room is large and airy, but being at the side of the house it does not get as much light as some of the others. Today the sun is shining though, so the two large windows allow the dappled sunlight which penetrates through the dark trees to enter the room. I am just about to take my place at my desk, when I hear a stifled cough, looking round I cannot see where it could have come from. So, telling myself it must have come from another room, I sit down and begin to read through my plan for today's lessons. Again I hear a stifled cough, and this time I know it comes from somewhere inside this room. Getting up for my chair I look all around the room until eventually my eyes catch sight of a heavy velvet drape in one corner. It is only the width of a door and I had seen it when I entered, but assumed that it was just disguising a cupboard or possibly a large painting. Not wanting to pry I had ignored it, but now find myself quietly and a little apprehensively walking towards it, stopping before opening it to listen. I can hear someone crying but am unsure whether to enter and see who it is and try and discover what is wrong, or whether to find Lady Elizabeth. Looking back at the large clock I realise that my young students will arrive in only ten minutes time. I decide I will have to investigate myself, carefully pulling back the heavy drape, I discover another much smaller but brighter room. Sitting in the small window seat is a small waif-like child with jet-black hair which gleams in the sunlight. She is unaware of my presence at first as she is hugging her knees tightly and her head is bowed forward resting on them. She is curled up so tightly that I am only a few feet away before she raises her head and notices me coming towards her. When she realises that she has been discovered her expression changes to one of total terror. I recognise her face as the same one that was looking out at me the day I arrived at Benfleet Hall.

`Miss Ruth, are you alright? Don't be afraid I am not going to give you away, if you want to stay you can, we will be in the big room so you won't be disturbed.'

She stops crying and Miss Ruth, for that is who she is, looks at me trying to decide whether to run away or stay in her secret hiding place. I move back so that she is not feeling threatened, this seems to put her more at ease.

`Would you like some paper with some writing and drawing utensils? You can use them in here while we are next door, and if you would like to show me later what you have done I would love to see your work.'

Deciding I am not going to get a response, I decide to collect some materials and leave them for her anyway. I am very aware that my three young students must not know of Miss Ruth's presence, so I return promptly to the big room taking great care to draw the curtain fully behind me.

My three young students arrive promptly appearing eager to learn and to please me. This morning's lessons seem to go well with time passing so quickly that it is soon time for lunch. I dismiss the three girls explaining that I will join them shortly but I have to clear things away ready for this afternoon. I also want to check on Miss Ruth without alerting anyone else to her presence. Once my preparations for afternoon lessons are complete, I quietly approach and pull back the drape to allow myself access to the smaller room. Miss Ruth sees me immediately and tries to hide what she has been working on.

`Please, Miss Ruth do not hide away what you have done, I really am interested and would love to see it. I would like to be your friend and help you too if you will let me?'

At first her reluctance to show me is great, but as I turn to leave, I hear it, the faintest of whispers, but she is definitely calling me back. Trying to hide my delight so that I don't do anything that will cause her to stop, I turn slowly asking again to see what she has done this morning. Slowly and timidly she turns the paper over to reveal the most beautiful drawing of a young woman, not much older than myself tenderly cradling her new baby girl. I can feel tears welling up inside me as I know at once that Miss Ruth has produced a portrait of her mother.

`This is beautiful Miss Ruth; you obviously enjoy art and have a great talent for it.'

A smile flickers across her chalk-pale face, and I now know how I can help this fragile child back towards happiness and a relationship with her heart-broken father.

`Would you like to do some more this afternoon? We will be in the big room again from half past two until four o'clock, but no-one but me need know you are here.'

Her expression changes for the first time into one of pure joy, so I collect further materials for her before going down to lunch. As I turn to leave there is again a whisper, this time I hear clearly.

`Thank you Miss.'

Not daring to turn round or respond for fear of showing my feelings, I leave the room knowing things here at Benfleet Hall are already changing for the better.

To my surprise when I reach the dining room Sir Abraham has decided to join us for lunch today, and beckons to me to take a seat beside him. Feeling rather apprehensive I do as I am bid.

`Miss Isabella, I have not yet spent any time getting to know you, and for that I can only apologise. I understand that Lady Phoebe has made you aware of the unhappy circumstances surrounding our family and I appreciate that your family life and childhood has not always been happy either. I am also aware that your father may still pose a risk to your safety, please be assured that we are doing and will continue to do all we can to keep you safe from any danger. I do hope you will consider yourself to be part of our family, despite being employed as governess and tutor to our three young daughters, and that you will enjoy your time here with us. As you know my older daughter, Miss Ruth rarely leaves her room, but I do hope that you will be prepared to meet her with me one day soon, although please do not expect too much in return, she speaks to no-one, not even me. Now let us eat before lunch is spoiled.'

I am quite taken aback but what has just occurred, and decide that perhaps I should ask to speak privately to Sir Abraham after lunch, before commencing the afternoon lessons.

With lunch complete I decide to seize my opportunity.

`Sir Abraham, may I speak with you in private before I return to the school room?'

` Why of course Miss Isabella, I do hope there is nothing wrong. Please follow me to the drawing room; we shall not be disturbed in there.'

I follow him as instructed taking a seat opposite him so that we are able to talk in comfort.

`What is it Miss Isabella? How can I help? Is there something causing you a problem?'

With my anxiety building, I pause and take a deep breath before I answer him.

`No Sir, there is no problem, everyone

has welcomed me very warmly and your daughters are delightful, very eager to learn and to please me, making my job much easier and more enjoyable.'

`Then what is it? Please be at ease to tell me anything that is on your mind.'

`Thank you. It is about Miss Ruth that I need to speak to you. I need to explain that we have already met. On my arrival at the school room this morning, I discovered the door was already open but could see no-one in the room. Thinking nothing more about it I completed my preparations for the morning lessons. Just as I was about to take my seat and read through my lesson plan again I heard a stifled cough, seeing no-one I assumed it was coming from another room. Having been sitting for a few minutes I heard it again, and this time I knew it was from within that room. With only a short while before Sarah, Mary and Harriet arrived for their lessons, I had to investigate the source.'

At this point Sir Abraham's expression changes from one of concern to one of weariness and anguish.

`Miss Isabella, you discovered Miss Ruth behind the curtain in the small room didn't you?'

Relieved that he has guessed I continue to explain what has occurred, and when I tell him what she has produced and that she spoke, his eyes are brimming over with tears. I also explain that she is intending to do more this afternoon if this is acceptable, and that I would dearly love to teach her too but separate from the three younger ones.

`I believe I can help her to find her life again, and would really value the opportunity to try she has an artistic gift that needs to be nurtured.'

A smile spreads across Sir Abraham's face and the tears appear in his eyes before slowly trickling down his face.

`I believe you can and please teach her as you will, you have my blessing. If you can give me my daughter back and restore peace and harmony to our fractured family you will have given me the miracle I have longed for throughout many years and I will owe you everything.'

`Thank you Sir, but I require nothing in return, I just want the chance to give someone else who is hurting as I did the chance to recover and live again in joy.'

The meeting with Sir Abraham had been much easier and more positive than I could have dared to imagine. Returning to the school room this afternoon I am filled with a new confidence and sense of purpose. Mary, Sarah and Harriet arrive early and are keen to learn anything I teach them. The girls finish and leave promptly at four o'clock enabling me to return to Miss Ruth in the small room, but before I reach the curtain she is already standing in front of me in the main room. She is clutching another beautiful picture in her right-hand, this time of her three sisters.

`Come in Miss Ruth, take a seat, I wish to talk to you, please don't be afraid.'
Timidly and very slowly Miss Ruth sits herself at a desk, watching my every move as though she is trying to assess me in some way.

`Miss Ruth, I have spoken at some length with your father and told him of the precious gift you possess with art, and he has willingly agreed that I should tutor you as well as your sisters.'
Fear appears in the dark eyes of this hurting, vulnerable child, and I know exactly how she is feeling, having been just as frightened many times in my life.

`Please don't fret child, you can be taught alone if this is what you wish, I can time your lessons to fit between those of your sisters. Would you like me to teach you?'
Miss Ruth says nothing, but holds out her hand to me, I offer her mine and she takes it so gently, then with tears in her eyes she nods her head and pushes her second picture of the day towards me. With a lump in my throat I take it and look more closely, now I can see that there are in fact four girls in the picture

not three. Miss Ruth had included herself but only at a distance from her sisters. This image breaks my heart as I know at once it is her way of saying how isolated and alone she feels.

`Miss Ruth is your ability to read and write at the same high level as your art?'
I hope for a response, but decide to offer her paper, writing materials and one of my favourite books from my childhood. Eagerly she takes all three, and taking the pot of ink and the writing nib she begins to show me how talented she really is.

When we eventually leave the school room two hours later, she has written the most beautiful yet tragic story in the most elegant hand I have ever seen. With her permission, I take both pictures and the story to her father's study after dinner.

`Sir Abraham, I am terribly sorry to disturb you, but I have Miss Ruth's permission to show you what she has achieved today.'

`Come in Miss Isabella, please sit down, I simply cannot believe you have succeeded in gaining her trust so quickly. '

`Sir, I think perhaps because I too have felt emotional pain, isolation and fear I am able to approach her in a way that nobody else can.'

`You may well be right. Although I

know she always loved to be with her mother while she painted, I had no idea that she had an interest in art herself, or even remembered those times so clearly, she was so tiny.'

Handing him the two small pictures and the story, I watch this man become more at peace and alive than I could have hoped for.

I leave the study and go up to my room with the knowledge that barriers are being broken down. For the first time in my life I am needed and can make a difference to the lives of those around me. This entire family has become very precious to me already, but my work here has only just begun and now I have two lots of lessons to plan. I am still working when the clock downstairs strikes midnight, but I decide that I must go to bed or I will be unable to perform my duties in the morning. It is with real hope and fulfilment that I turn out my lamp tonight, tomorrow will be a challenge, but one which really thrills me.

After my late night, I wake later than usual this morning, leaving me feeling rushed and slightly ill-prepared as I hurry down to breakfast. The three young sisters and Lady Elizabeth are already seated; as is Sir Abraham, but as I enter the room and see Miss Ruth sitting beside her father my heart leaps, seeing me she beckons me to the seat next to her. I look to Sir Abraham for approval, but there is no need, the delight on his face says all I need to know.

`Sorry I am late this morning; I was working until late and couldn't wake myself at my usual time.'

`Miss Isabella, please do not worry yourself, there is no rush, and to ensure you have some time to yourself, Lady Elizabeth and I have agreed that Mary, Sarah and Harriet will be taught in the morning and Miss Ruth in the afternoon. Will that suit you?'

`Why thank you Sir, are the girls happy with this arrangement?'

`They are, also you are to have every other weekend off so that you may visit Havergal Manor if you wish, or just spend your time writing the poetry which I understand you love and are very gifted at. Will this fulfil your needs?'

`This is more than adequate, thank you Sir you are most generous, but if any of the girls should need me, please allow me to be there for them. I enjoy the company of all four, and for the first time in my life, know what my purpose is. Thank you all for making me so welcome and I hope my service to your family will continue to meet with your approval.'

`Miss Isabella, we truly cannot begin to thank you enough, since your arrival here at Benfleet Hall. Our fractured, wounded family

is beginning to rebuild its bridges. We owe
you so much, what we offer in return is the
least that you are due.'

Unable to speak, as I know I will give way to
my emotions, I nod my head and finish my
breakfast quickly so that I can make my
escape to the school room.

Here I start to prepare the lessons for the
three younger girls, no longer having to fight
to keep my tears inside. My life is now so
good and comfortable, I am terrified that it
won't last and dare not allow myself to even
think about my future.

At this time I have duties to perform and a
roll to play and knowing this is enough.

By the time the girls arrive, I have calmed
myself down. I am looking forward to today
and am just going to enjoy my present good
fortune for as long as it lasts.

My joy is great,
My hope is strong,
Am I at last where I belong?
Imparting knowledge,
To eager minds,
Enjoying a life,
I once so longed for.
Fulfilling a promise,
Made three years ago,
To someone I can no longer see,
But still miss so much each new day,

**Mother, your presence is with me I know,
Wherever I go, I carry you too.**

***

I arrived at Benfleet Hall barely a month ago, and already so much has happened. Having been appointed as governess to three very young sisters, after only twenty-four hours, I find myself governess and tutor to four girls, the oldest of which I had hoped for but not expected, and certainly not so soon after my arrival. I have not yet returned to Havergal Manor, but this weekend is my weekend off so arrangements have been made for me to go then. November has arrived and with it the first of the winter snowfall, hence the reason my visit is to take place now before the weather closes in and the journey becomes almost impossible and quite hazardous. Winters here are hard and long, but for the first time in my life I am not dreading either winter or Christmas. I feel safe, loved and most fulfilling of all, really needed by people who already mean a great deal to me.

I am very aware that it is wrong to have favourites where children are concerned, but Miss Ruth reminds me so much of myself when I first arrived at Havergal Manor that I find that I am drawn to her particularly. It is so encouraging to see the progress she is making with her studies, and the relationship between her and Sir Abraham is growing by the day. She still prefers to be taught apart from her sisters and very rarely speaks, but I know that given time this will also change.

Preparations for Christmas are now well underway and although it is only the beginning of November, because of how the weather deteriorates as the weeks pass, plans have to be made early with food and other supplies being bought so that travel through the worst of winter is not necessary. I have been given the choice as to whether I remain here for Christmas or return to Havergal Manor, but because of how long the worst of the weather can last, I will be remaining here at Benfleet Hall. I would not want to have to delay my return to my duties as governess, as I feel the progress Miss Ruth is making must be allowed to continue. Any prolonged gap in her current routine may hinder this, and it is not fair on her to have to start again.

Mary, Sarah and Harriet are still very eager, and despite Harriet being two years younger than her sisters, her ability to absorb and retain her lessons is certainly equal to that of her sisters. On some occasions her concentration is better than her two older siblings, who are inclined to either drift into daydreams or else get a fit of the giggles. I manage to regain their attention however, I simply ask them to recite either a poem or some other excerpt of literature which they have learned earlier in their time with me, as both like to show off slightly this works for both them and me. Sarah appears to really enjoy poetry, so I try to allow time each day for her to start trying to write her own. Mary on the other hand seems to prefer to continue with her needlework when time allows, although as I say both read and recite poetry and other small excerpts of literature beautifully and eloquently. Harriet always seems to enjoy learning whatever I prepare for her lessons, but music seems to be her passion, so I have spoken at length with Lady Elizabeth about the possibility of her learning to play the piano next year. It would mean another tutor coming in to provide this tuition, as I was never able to learn until I arrived at Havergal Manor, so do not know enough to teach her myself. Lady Elizabeth has agreed to talk to Sir Abraham and look into this possibility. I can teach them simple songs to sing, but feel inadequate to even do this properly. A music tutor, I believe, would be a benefit to all four girls, including Miss Ruth.

My own tutor, Miss Grace, had taught me well in many areas including basic music and piano, but not to a level where I feel confident enough to teach anyone else. Sir Abraham has spoken to a music tutor who has agreed to start teaching the girls on a weekly basis from April next year. The three younger girls are all very excited, but Miss Ruth has indicated to me that she does not wish to be taught by somebody she does not know. I have tried to explain to her that no-one is going to force her, but I have suggested that perhaps she may like to sit in when one of her sisters is having a lesson and listen, perhaps while doing some silent reading or painting so that she is concentrating on something instead of feeling insecure or panicked, or even that she is in the way. She has agreed to think about this and seems less anxious.

**

Today it has been arranged for me to pay my first visit to Havergal Manor since I left five weeks ago. Lord Sebastian is to collect me at noon on Saturday and I am to stay overnight and then return at noon on Sunday enabling me to resume my duties on Monday morning. Lady Elizabeth has told me that Miss Amelia is very excited, and Lady Phoebe is looking forward to hearing all my news. Miss Ruth does not want me to go, but I have assured her that I am coming back, and she needs to keep an eye on her sisters for me. At first this seems to alarm her greatly as she is only just beginning to get to know them, but when I explain that they really do want to be her friends and that if she helps them with their art she will be helping me, she agrees almost excitedly. She has no concept of time so even though I say I will be back tomorrow, the fact that I am away overnight, to her means I am leaving. My hope is that she will grow to understand, once she gets used to them, that my visits back to Havergal Manor are only temporary.

***

Today is Saturday, and the day that Lord Sebastian arrives to take me back to Havergal Manor for the first time since I took up my new position as a governess and tutor. Feeling happy and secure, I am up early and arrive downstairs for breakfast before Lady Elizabeth or any of the family. Not expecting to find anyone in the dining room, I enter as always and head towards the table to take my seat, and wait for the family to join me. But before I have taken two steps inside the room I discover that I am not alone. There is a tall dark-haired young man standing with his back to me gazing out of the window, as I have not yet met him and being aware that he only arrived back at Benfleet Hall yesterday, I know at once that he is Master Benedict.

`Oh! Excuse me; I was unaware that anyone else was in here. I am so early that I believed I was first.'

Master Benedict turns to face me, and at once I feel strange warmth rising up within me.

`That is quite alright Miss, you did not disturb me, allow me to introduce myself. I am Benedict, Sir Abraham's nephew, and you must be Miss Isabella. I am so pleased to make your acquaintance at last.'

Trying hard to catch my breath, I curtsy respectfully and return his most gracious introduction.

`Yes, I am indeed Miss Isabella, and I am very pleased to make your acquaintance too, Sir.'

Feeling awkward and vulnerable, I am very relieved when it is not long before we are joined by the rest of the family, and breakfast is soon over. Before I can leave the room however, Master Benedict catches me by the hand and asks me to stay behind so that we may get to know each other better.

`Miss Isabella, why the rush to leave? Do you not enjoy my company? Come, take a seat with me in the window, so that we can talk and get properly acquainted with each other.'

Feeling shy and very unsure, I try to make my excuses and once again turn to leave, but something inside me is preventing me from moving further.

`If you please Master Benedict, I am to be collected at noon today by Lord Sebastian for my first visit to Havergal Manor since I took up my post here. I really must go and prepare my things which I need to take with me, as I am not returning until noon tomorrow.'

A beautifully entrancing smile appears on this handsome, gentle-featured face causing a twinkle to appear in his kind, warm eyes. I begin to feel light-headed and giddy, but not in an unpleasant way. What is happening to me? I have never felt like this before. Unable to fight, I find myself being led to the large window seat at the far end of the dining room.

`Miss Isabella, are you frightened of me? I can assure you that I mean you no harm, I simply find you enchanting company.'

A flicker of mild concern mixed with a little amusement dances across the face now looking intently at me.

`No Sir, of course not, but I really do need to gather my thoughts, and things for my visit together before Lord Sebastian's arrival.'

`And so you shall, but please promise me that when you return tomorrow, you and I may talk and learn about each other properly.'

Unsure of how to respond, I agree, but I know in my mind and in my heart, that this situation is something I must talk about with Lady Phoebe during my time at the Manor this weekend. I leave the dining room quickly and head to the safe security of my own room.

Sitting in my own window seat, having completed the preparations for my visit, I look out onto the snowy garden below. I try to make sense of this morning's events, but the harder I try to understand the more confused and uncertain I feel. I am still sitting here when there is a knock at my door.

`Come in.'

Lady Elizabeth enters to inform me that Lord Sebastian has just arrived, and to make my way to the drawing room when I am ready.

`Miss Isabella, is there anything you need to take with you that you cannot carry?'

`My valise is not light, I should be grateful if someone could carry it down for me. Thank you, Lady Elizabeth you are to kind.'

`I shall send someone to collect it immediately.'

Two minutes later, there is a knock at my door, and Master Benedict appears. His velvet voice sends a shiver down my spine, and I am sure I am blushing. I fear I may know now what I am feeling, could I be falling in love?

`I have come to collect your valise, Miss Isabella. Allow me to escort you to the drawing room, please take my arm.'

With my valise in his right hand, and my hand holding timidly to his left arm, we descend the stairs together, but before entering the room I drop my hand to my side and refuse to let him take it again.

We leave Benfleet Hall almost immediately, so that our arrival at Havergal Manor can be before any further snow falls and the light begins to fade. The journey is cold but quite thrilling, and I cannot wait to see everyone again. As we enter the large wrought iron gates and start up the long gravel drive, Havergal Manor comes into view and I am flooded with a real sense of coming home.

On our arrival Lady Phoebe greets me at the door, and unlike my initial arrival three years earlier, Miss Amelia is not starring out of her window, but running down the hall ready to grab me in an enthusiastic embrace. But on seeing Lord Sebastian's disapproval she slows her pace and walks towards me, before embracing me as though I had been gone five years, not five weeks.

`Miss Amelia, please allow Miss Isabella to get through the door! She is here until tomorrow, so there will be plenty of time later on for you to catch up.'

`I'm sorry Sir, but I have been quite lonely and I am just so pleased to see my friend again.'

`I know you are, but manners and etiquette must be maintained.'

`Sebastian, she is doing no harm. Come straight through into the dining room all of you, lunch is ready.'

`I apologise my love, you are right of course, but young ladies must be encouraged to behave as such, not like uneducated adolescent girls who are allowed to run wild and know no better. Miss Amelia I am sorry that I raised my voice, but try to remember what is acceptable behaviour in the future.'

`Yes Sir.'

The hot soup is most welcome after our carriage journey through the intensely cold winter weather, and I am able to relax immediately. I know however, that I must find time to talk to Lady Phoebe about Master Benedict, and the sooner the better. His position in the family is that of a nephew, mine is only that of governess and tutor to the four young daughters. He is also in training to become a clergyman and as such I am very unsure of the duties of a vicar's wife. A relationship between us seems in my mind completely out of the question, and yet I cannot deny what I feel. If my presence at Benfleet Hall is going to cause problems then I must not return tomorrow, and must request my belongings be returned to me. I do not want this to happen but I see no other choice. Lady Phoebe will be able to advise me, and I know she will listen to what I need to say. I must speak to her today.

I am very aware that Miss Amelia is desperate for me to spend time with her, so that we can talk and catch up, but I must speak to Lady Phoebe first and alone.

`Lady Phoebe, may I speak with you after lunch, it is very important and really cannot wait. '

`Why, of course Isabella, are you alright? All the reports we have had regarding your progress have been outstanding. Lord Abraham is so appreciative and grateful for the work you are doing with Miss Ruth; he is beginning to believe that his daughter will soon become the fun-loving happy child that she once was. Is there something wrong? Are you unhappy?'

Her heart-felt concern for me is obvious for all to see, and Miss Amelia looks as though she is about to burst into tears.

`I am quite well thank you Lady Phoebe, and thoroughly enjoying my work. The four girls are all delightful, eager to learn and to please me. I really feel that I am needed and can make a valuable contribution to the lives of all those at Benfleet Hall. But I really do not wish to or feel that I can say more until we are alone.'

At this Miss Amelia looks hard at me, and I fear I know what she is going to say.

`Miss Isabella, I am your friend, do you

not trust me enough to let me in on your secret or to help you?'

Seeing the hurt in her eyes, I know that she is also genuinely concerned for me, and decide that when I have spoken to Lady Phoebe and decisions have been made, I must share my news with my friend, even if I am unable to share all the details.

`Please Miss Amelia, try to be patient with me, I will tell you when I can, but I must seek advice first. I must tell someone who can help me make the right decision. Lady Phoebe can give me the answers that I seek, as well as the guidance and reassurance that I need.'

`Don't upset yourself Isabella, come to the drawing room immediately after lunch, and we will talk undisturbed for as long as you need to. Miss Amelia please do as Isabella has asked you, when she is ready I will collect you myself so that you can join us in the drawing room.'

Lunch is soon finished, as arranged Lady Phoebe and I retire to the drawing room. I go to take up my usual seat opposite Lady Phoebe, but today she comes over, takes hold of my hands and sits beside me.

`Now Isabella, take your time and tell me everything you need to. Please do not be frightened or ashamed, you are an attractive young woman now, and are bound to attract the attention of young gentlemen.'

This statement surprises me greatly, does she already know what I am about to say?

'Lady Phoebe, how did you know what I need to talk to you about?'

'Dear Isabella, it was only a matter of time before such a set of circumstances arose, and I recognised the look of feeling different inside the very minute you arrived here today. If you had not asked to speak to me, I would have asked you here this afternoon anyway. Affairs of the heart can be confusing and hard to cope with, especially if you have never experienced these feelings before, but they are perfectly natural and expected for girls your age. Now, start from the beginning and try not to upset yourself.'

I take a deep breath in an attempt to calm myself, before trying to explain something which I still do not understand myself.

'As you know Lady Phoebe, Sir Abraham has a nephew who is training as a clergyman to take up his appointment at the chapel which is attached to the Benfleet estate. He has to spend much of his time away, but when he returns he resides at the Hall. Yesterday Master Benedict arrived back, and is due to remain until after Christmas. I did not see him when he arrived last night as it was late, but I was up for breakfast early this morning. I wanted to be ready for Lord Sebastian, and was so looking forward to seeing everyone; I was not able to sleep. On my arrival at the dining room, I thought at first that I was alone, but then I saw him, standing with his back to me looking out of the window. I apologise immediately for disturbing him. As he turns to face me, he assures me that that my presence is not a disturbance to him and proceeds to introduce himself. He already appears to know who I am and takes my hand kissing it so gently that I begin to feel very awkward. Curtsying respectfully, and trying to catch my breath, I return his most gracious introduction and confirm that I am indeed Miss Isabella.

The initial awkwardness does not last long as we are soon joined by the rest of the family. Their appearance is such a relief to me and breakfast is soon well underway. However, when it is over, before I am able to leave the room, Master Benedict catches me by my hand wanting to know why I am in such a hurry to leave, and whether I disliked his company. He invites me to join him in the window seat so that we may get properly acquainted. I try to make my excuses by explaining that I must be ready to be collected for my visit here. I turn once again and try to leave, but something inside me is preventing me from taking another step.'

A knowing, yet kindly smile appears on Lady Phoebe's face, and she gently squeezes my hands reassuringly.

`Isabella, please go on.'

I can feel myself trembling all over and by the heat I can feel in my cheeks, I know that I am blushing, so I take another deep breath before I continue.

`He looks at me, and the smile on his face is entrancing and beautiful all at the same time, and this smile causes his kind, warm eyes to twinkle. His face is handsome, with such gentle features and I cannot fight him anymore. Feeling light-headed and giddy, I allow myself to be led by the hand to the window seat. Once we are seated he then asks me if I am frightened of him, and I can see in his eyes that this is a real concern for him, his assurances that he means me no harm are so heart-felt that I know he means every word. He then tells me that he finds my company enchanting. I try to assure him that he does not frighten me, but again explain that I must ensure that I am ready to depart at noon.

Releasing my hand he tells me I may go, but makes me promise that I will speak with him on my return. When I am back in the safe security of my own room I start to try to make sense of what had just take place, but I become even more confused and uncertain the more I think about it. Then when Lady Elizabeth says that someone will be up to collect my valise, it is he who appears. His rich, deep, velvet voice sends a shiver down my spine and I know I must be blushing, so I turn away trying to hide my face from him.

Oh Lady Phoebe, I think I may be falling in love with him. What am I going to do? I cannot tell him of my background with all its horrors, and my position as governess and tutor is so important to me, I do not want to give it up. If I leave Benfleet Hall, I feel as though I would be deserting the girls, especially Miss Ruth who really seems to be starting to trust me. She has made such progress, and I have promised her that I will return tomorrow. But I am so aware of his position in the family and in wider society, that I know any relationship with him is impossible. Please help me! With him still there, how can I possibly go back tomorrow?'
The tears that were pricking my eyes are now flowing freely, and Lady Phoebe is once again sitting stroking my hair comfortingly, as I rest my head on her shoulder. She has done this so often when I was younger, I feel like that hurting, frightened child again, but this time the reasons are so very different.

`Isabella, there is no reason why you are less entitled to happiness than anyone else. As you know Lady Elisabeth herself began her own life at Benfleet Hall as a Nanny to Miss Ruth after the death of her mother. Your background before your life here is of no importance, this was the reason for your new identity when you first came to us.

Would you like me to accompany you when you return tomorrow? Then we can speak to Lady Elizabeth and Sir Abraham together, and put your concerns to them. But I am sure they will be as delighted for you and Benedict as I am and Lord Sebastian will be when we tell him. You are a loyal and beautiful young lady, and after your very difficult start in life, you deserve some real happiness and the genuine love of a man who is kind and gentle. Master Benedict is a sweet-natured and gentle man, he too had an early life full of trauma and heartache, so both of you deserve a future filled with hope and true love. As you are only eighteen, we as your guardians will have to give our consent, but rest assured you will have that and our blessing.'

After taking tea alone with Lady Phoebe, Miss Amelia was collected and came to join us in the drawing room. She is desperate to know what we have been talking about, but Lady Phoebe has advised me to keep details brief at this stage, at least until after tomorrow.

`Miss Amelia, I cannot say too much at the moment, but I am asking you to be pleased for me. I have had the pleasure of being introduced to a very charming and handsome young man, or I should say he introduced himself only this morning just before breakfast. I do not know what the future holds at this time, but I think I have already fallen in love with him. Everything feels so different, strange and confusing at the moment, but it also feels so right and thrilling. I cannot say more at the moment as Lady Elizabeth and Sir Abraham do not know as yet, unless he has spoken to them. What I will say is that his name is Benedict and he is training to be a clergyman.'

Miss Amelia's reaction is one of surprise and excitement mixed with a little uncertainty that quickly turns into one of anger.

`Miss Isabella, how can you possibly know what you feel after only one brief introduction? Am I to lose my friend forever? I cannot deny that I am thrilled for you, but if your future life is to be with him, will I ever see you? If you should get married, can I be your maid of honour? Oh, I really don't know what to say, or how to feel.'

I am concerned for my friend as Lady Phoebe tries to calm her down and help her to understand, but then Miss Amelia's whole expression changes. Her next remark is so sharp and viciously spoken, I feel as though my heart has been pierced with an arrow.

`This is not fair, I too am eighteen and crave to be loved by a gentleman, how can you do this to me? I want no more to do with you or your future life! I thought we were real friends, and would do everything together; first you leave me here alone to take up a position as a governess and tutor, and now this. Don't you care about me at all? Don't you want to be friends with me anymore? I never thought you could be so selfish!'

Miss Amelia moves quickly to leave the room, leaving me heart-broken and in tears, but Lady Phoebe reaches the door before her, blocking her path.

`Miss Amelia, this outburst is quite unnecessary, and it is certainly unacceptable and unseemly for young ladies. You will return to your seat and apologise to Miss Isabella at once! She will never abandon you or your friendship, and she most definitely is not selfish.'

Seeing the surprised look on both my face and that of Miss Amelia, Lady Phoebe softens her tone again and continues.

`Your time will come Amelia, but these things cannot be forced. They happen naturally and when the time is right, not just because we want them too. Miss Isabella never intended for this to happen, and certainly not so soon or so quickly. None of this is her fault, and she has not done it with the intention of hurting anyone.'

Then taking Miss Amelia's hands in hers she continues, but this time much more gently, and far more like the Lady Phoebe we have both known and loved since our individual arrivals at Havergal Manor.

`I had no idea that you felt so alone since Isabella left us to take up her position at Benfleet Hall. Why did you not tell me sooner? You know I am always here for you.'

`Oh, Lady Phoebe, until Miss Isabella arrived today, I had not realized how lonely I was. Then when she was so happy and told me her special news, I felt as though she was leaving all over again. I am still happy for her, but then I became frightened because I began to think I will never know this same happiness myself and it hurts.

Miss Isabella can you ever forgive me, I did not mean any of what I said. I don't really want to lose your friendship or your company. You are the only true friend I have ever had and I am scared that if you marry, I will be forgotten.'

`Miss Amelia, I could never forget you, you stood by me and gave me new hope and belief in a better life when everything in my world was black and threatening. Marriage could be a long way off yet, and we would not be too far apart, as he is to take up his post as vicar to the Benfleet Hall Estate. The vicarage is only about two miles from Benfleet

Hall. But all of this is very much uncertain and nothing is decided. This is all in the very distant future. As I am only here until tomorrow please let us enjoy our short time together.'

Many tears have been shed this afternoon, and with dinner in less than an hour, I ask to be excused. I am to share Miss Amelia's room again tonight, for the first time since moving to Benfleet Hall, I will have company at night. I retire to our room to compose myself and freshen up before dinner, but know I must give myself time to write the poems that are dancing round my head. One is for Amelia to show her how much she is loved and cared for by me, the other is for me. I need to put into words I am feeling and everything that has happened today. This is the only way I know how to escape from reality and look at things differently. I do not know or understand why writing poetry helps; I have just learned over the last three years that it does.

When your rich, velvet voice spoke my name,
You unlocked the key to my love,
My heart had been captured that instant,
I knew I would never again feel the same.
Your eyes are so gentle,
They show me you're kind,

I know from that moment,
I love you.
The shiver down my spine,
When with such tenderness,
You kiss my hand,
A flutter in my heart,
My breathless, light-headed delight,
When I first saw you standing,
In the early morn light,
I knew from that moment,
I love you.

Time has flown by, and as I make my way back downstairs for dinner, I decide that I will write Miss Amelia's poem and leave it for her when I depart tomorrow. To return to her room and find it waiting for her, will, I hope go some small way to building a bridge between us, and help her realise how special she is to me. I am anxious as I approach the dining room, will she still be resentful of me? Has Lady Phoebe spoken with Lord Sebastian yet? Can I really be looking at a future with a man who is so kind, gentle and loves me without boundaries? My life is so different now from the one I left behind as a frightened child just three years ago, and back then none of this even seemed possible.

My concerns regarding Miss Amelia and Lord Sebastian were about as far from reality as they could be. Before I even reach the door of the dining room, Miss Amelia has grabbed my arm and is back to the excitable girl that had greeted me when I arrived earlier that day. Lord Sebastian says nothing as we enter the dining room, however, once we are all seated he stands and says grace and then, looking at me and smiling makes an announcement.

`It is with gladness and joy that we are able to once again share a meal with Miss Isabella, and we are so happy that she has found happiness and fulfilment in her life after such a traumatic and difficult childhood.

Both Lady Phoebe and I will accompany her when she returns to Benfleet Hall tomorrow, to speak with Sir Abraham and Lady Elizabeth. Following this meeting we hope we will be able to make plans for a real celebration. So, Miss Isabella, I would like to say how glad we both are that your future is looking so much more secure and filled with happiness. It has been a real joy to be able to play some small part in putting right a wrong, and fulfilling the dying wish of a lady who was so precious to both you and I.'

As he retakes his seat so that we are able to start dinner, I can feel the tears starting to fall. Unable to hold back, I look to him and offer my thanks and appreciation for everything that has been done for me.

`Lord Sebastian, Lady Phoebe, I owe

you so much and cannot begin to thank you for what you have done for me. But please rest assured that I will continue to always look for opportunities in which I may be able to help others who are suffering, escape from their trials and live the life they deserve.'

Dinner continues with the usual polite conversation, and at the end we all retire to the drawing room. But as the evening progresses, although tired I do not want to leave. Today has been an incredible mixture of excitement, confusion and so many other feelings and emotions, I do not want it to end, yet I do so want to see Benedict again tomorrow. I still dare not believe that this could be happening to me, it is like living in a dream.

By the time the clock in the hall strikes eleven I have to make my excuses and leave to go to bed. My eyes are so heavy they now refuse to stay open, and tomorrow is going to be busy. And I still have to write Miss Amelia's poem. But now I need to sleep. Miss Amelia catches me up before I reach the bedroom and we both tumble into our beds and drift off to sleep almost instantly.

***

I awake this morning to find snow is falling again and am concerned about my return journey to Benfleet Hall. It is still early so I dress quickly and quietly trying not to wake

Miss Amelia, so that I can write her poem before breakfast. But she is already stirring, so I begin gathering my belongings together so I am ready to leave at noon.

At breakfast I decide to voice my concerns regarding the weather and ask if Lord Sebastian would rather leave earlier. He assures me that there is no rush and that the weather has been far worse than it is today. Gazing out of the window I find that hard to believe, but I trust him and can use the time to write Miss Amelia's poem. She is desperate that we should spend our remaining time today together. But eventually I manage to persuade her that if she allows me an hour to myself, the last hour before I leave, can be devoted entirely to her.

Returning to the bedroom after breakfast I first ensure that my valise is packed and ready for our departure at noon. This task complete I can now concentrate on Miss Amelia's poem.

On the day that I arrived,
Friendless, frightened, alone,
Your face appeared at a window,
Giving me hope that a friendship might grow.
It took us time,
At first we just smiled,
At mealtimes over the table.

Everything changed on that one night,
When two visitors came to my room,
One after the other,
Both gave me a fright,
But you gave me a reason to hope.
You told me your story,
Being new here yourself,
We found we could help each other to cope,
Then when Meg died,
I felt so alone,
And my father still posed such a threat.
But you were there through it all,
Never turning your back,
On a friend so forlorn and at risk.
The friendship we have,
Has a bond so secure,
And is based on such a great love,
That no matter where either one of us goes,
The other can blossom,
In the knowledge and trust,
We are together forever in spirit.
So whenever you miss me,
Or I miss you,
We will each pick a rose,
Or some other flower,
And send it down stream,
With love for each other.

I have only just finished writing when there is
a knock on my door.
        `Who is it?'

Scrabbling around for an envelope in which to hide the poem, I await a response. I find an envelope and placing the poem inside I lay it carefully on her pillow. Then instead of a response, there is another knock.

`Who is it? Is it you Miss Amelia?'

`Yes it's me, are you ready yet? Please come and talk with me before you have to leave.'

Relieved to get an answer this time, I go to the door and the two of us go downstairs to the drawing room. We are still there when Lady Phoebe appears.

`Isabella, are you ready? We need to go now if Lord Sebastian and I are to get back here before darkness falls.'

`My valise, it's still upstairs!'

`No child it has been collected and is already in the carriage waiting for you. Say your goodbyes and come straight out, we are waiting for you.'

Seeing the look on Miss Amelia's face, I say nothing, but embrace her and kiss her cheek. I turn and leave the room without looking back. I hate leaving her all over again, but the difference this time is that I do it safe in the knowledge that I have said everything in the poem on her pillow.

The journey back to Benfleet Hall is bitterly cold and very difficult; the snow is still falling and showing no sign of stopping. My concern for Lord Sebastian and Lady Phoebe returning to Havergal Manor later in the day is great, but Lord Sebastian assures me that he would not have undertaken any journey unless he was certain of being able to return safely. As we turn onto the long drive, passing through the ornate gates that lead to Benfleet Hall, I begin to feel very nervous and unsure about the whole situation.

`Miss Isabella, are you feeling unwell? You have gone quite pale, what is wrong child?'

I knew that Lady Phoebe was perceptive, but being in the dimly lit carriage I was surprised that my feelings were so obvious.

`Oh, Lady Phoebe, I am so nervous, all that I have experienced and felt during the last two days is so new to me. I am frightened that it is not real, that I have dreamt or imagined it all. Worse still is that it is real, but will all go wrong and be snatched away from me.'

`Hush Isabella, all these feelings and thoughts are quite normal for a young lady suddenly finding herself in your position. Of course you are uncertain and anxious, but I can assure you that these feelings will ease and be replaced with joy, hope, happiness and most of all love.'

We arrive at the Hall and the carriage comes to a halt. Lady Elizabeth greets us at the door, and appears unsurprised at Lady Phoebe's presence.

`Please, come in all of you. Your journey must have been cold and difficult, there is hot soup waiting in the dining room for everyone. Phoebe, it is such a pleasure to see you again, and under such happy circumstances.'

Lady Phoebe makes no reply; instead she takes my hand and smiles knowingly in an attempt to reassure me.

Lunch is taken with the usual polite conversation being made around the table. The hot soup is warming me instantly from the inside in such a comforting way, that afterwards I could easily fall asleep. That is if it were not for the discussion that is to follow. As lunch draws to a conclusion, Sir Abraham invites us all to join him, Lady Elizabeth and Benedict in the drawing room.

As we leave the dining room and follow him through, my heart is pounding so hard I can barely breathe. Do they already know? Has Benedict told them? The discussion that is about to take place is going to change my life forever. To my surprise it is Lord Sebastian who is first to speak.

`Sir Abraham, Lady Elizabeth, before we start, myself and Lady Phoebe would like to express our sincere thanks for the way in which you have taken Miss Isabella into your home and into your hearts. We have noticed such a change in her this weekend, from the shy, timid girl who left us just five short weeks ago, she has blossomed into a confident, happy young woman, who has found a real purpose in her life. I know that Miss Isabella also wishes to express her gratitude for your kindness, so thank you from us all.'

`Lord Sebastian, Lady Phoebe, dear Isabella, you are all very kind and it is we who should be thanking you. Miss Isabella is such a joy to have as part of our household, and it is her presence here, coupled with her quiet, calm nature that has performed a miracle I never thought possible. She has restored my oldest daughter, Miss Ruth to me. Her dedication and loyalty are without question, and all four girls adore her. So I thank you for allowing her to come to us, and Miss Isabella I thank you for all you have done, and will, I hope continue to do for us and our daughters.

Now, it is with great pleasure that I share with you today, that my nephew Benedict has spoken with myself and Lady Elizabeth to explain how Miss Isabella has captured his heart. He wishes me to ask for your permission for him to ask Miss Isabella to do him the honour of becoming his wife. As you have both accompanied Miss Isabella today we hope that it is because she too has expressed feelings towards Benedict, and that there is no other reason for your visit.'

Lady Phoebe again takes hold of my hand, squeezing gently to reassure me. My heart is still pounding, but now with a thrill of expectation rather than fear. I am still very anxious and my shyness is evident to all, but I am so happy.

`Lady Phoebe and I are delighted to give our consent, and our blessing. To see Isabella looking forward to a life of hope and joy, filled with love, is, I know what her dear mother wanted for her and we are just delighted to have been able to provide her with this chance.'

Sir Abraham, Lady Elizabeth, Lord Sebastian and Lady Phoebe retire to the garden room, a large bright airy room at the rear of the Hall, leaving Benedict and I alone. My heart is racing and I can feel myself trembling all over, but when I look at Benedict he too seems nervous and insecure. Minutes go by before he finally speaks.

`Miss Isabella, since our all too brief introduction yesterday morning I have been unable to get your face out of my mind. You captured my heart instantly, and from that moment I knew I had to speak to my uncle. I was terrified, not of Sir Abraham, but of what I was feeling and of how uncle would react. I need not have been concerned, the instant I asked to speak with him alone, and he smiled and agreed as though he already knew why.

Miss Isabella, there is a question I must have an answer for today, and when I have asked, and you have given me your answer; we are to join the others.'

There is a silence before he speaks again, and the longer I sit waiting, the more I tremble. I never dared to believe that this day would come for me, and now it is here my head is in a whirl with none of my thoughts making any sense at all.

`Miss Isabella, from the first instant that my eyes saw you I knew deep in my heart that you were who I had been waiting for. I pray that you will consider what I ask carefully, and that your answer will be the one I desire. Miss Isabella, would you do me the great honour of becoming my wife?'

His eyes meet mine and now it is I who struggle to speak.

`Dear Benedict, your proposal was beautiful and I can scarcely believe that this is happening to me. Before I give you my answer, I must first tell you that when I left here yesterday for Havergal Manor, I was so confused and uncertain that I was unsure whether I should even return here today. I knew I had to speak to Lady Phoebe, but felt exactly as you did. The talk I had with her really helped, although travelling here today, I began doubting whether any of my feelings or memories of yesterday were even real. But to say that you have made me feel truly alive for the first time in my life is not an exaggeration. The answer to your question is yes, and I hope and pray that I will be as good a wife as you deserve.'

`Miss Isabella, you have just made me the happiest man alive, and I know that you will never let me down, my only hope is that I can be the husband that you deserve.'
Then offering me his arm and tenderly kissing my hand, he opens the door to the hallway.

`Shall we share this happy event with our two families so that we may all truly celebrate, before Lord Sebastian and Lady Phoebe have to make their very difficult return journey through the ever deepening snow? They need to return before daylight fades.'

Saying nothing, I take his arm willingly and together we make our way to join the others in the garden room. To my surprise, my four young students are also present when the formal announcement of our engagement is made, jointly by Sir Abraham and Lord Sebastian. Everyone seems to be delighted by this news, but the journey home which awaits Lord Sebastian and Lady Phoebe is concerning me greatly.

`Lady Phoebe and I thank you for your hospitality today, and are delighted to be able to return home with such good tidings. We must unfortunately make our excuses now and leave so we can arrive back at Havergal Manor before dark.'

`Will you be alright? The snow is getting thicker by the minute Lady Phoebe.'

`Now don't you fret Isabella we will be perfectly safe, I have seen and travelled through many winters worse than this one. Congratulations to you both, and we will see you again as soon as the weather breaks.'

Having said my goodbyes I watch until the carriage is no longer visible, and then return to the warmth of the garden room where talk continues until dinner.

***

The excitement of the weekend which drew to a wonderful conclusion with yesterday's announcement is still the main subject of everybody's conversation. My four students are no exception. The three younger girls, Sarah, Mary and Harriet are so caught up in the romance of it all, that their concentration during their lessons this morning is limited to say the least. After twenty minutes of continuous chatter and very little work, I decide to try a different approach.

`Girls I can appreciate that you are

excited, nobody can be more excited than I am, I am also very touched by your congratulations and good wishes for Benedict and I, but we cannot spend all our time talking about my engagement and forthcoming marriage. As your lessons this morning are literature and art, I wonder whether perhaps you might each like to focus your enthusiasm on drawing a picture of a bride on her wedding day, and then perhaps write a poem or a story to go with it. It could be about how she feels, what her hopes and dreams are for the future, and what her life was like before. You can imagine it whichever way you choose, but I do expect at least twenty minutes quiet work, so that you all have something to share at the end of lessons.'

Almost immediately the chattering stops and the girls begin to focus on producing some work, and seem to be really enjoying the tasks I have set them. This was not the subject I had planned for today, but if this focuses their attention back on their studies, then it is worthwhile and they are still learning and practising skills already learned.

By the time the morning is over and lunch is approaching, all three girls have produced a picture and a story. They are all very different, although each girl has shown real imagination and insight. I promise that I will read them before tomorrow and if they concentrate on the lessons I plan for tomorrow from the time they arrive, then perhaps we can finish a few minutes early and I will read each story out. They can hear each other's ideas then we may be able to talk about why they each see things so differently. This seems to find favour with all three; we all leave the school room and make our way downstairs to lunch.

This afternoon is my first opportunity to speak with Miss Ruth alone since my return yesterday. She arrives promptly for her lessons as always, but her usual enthusiasm is missing.

`Miss Ruth, are you alright? You do not seem yourself today, can I help.'

Her eyes look up at me with real sorrow in them, and she seems distant and removed, almost like she had been the day I first met her.

`I'm scared Miss Isabella. You are the only true friend I have ever known, and you really seem to understand my feelings of hurt and sorrow. I truly am pleased for you and my cousin, Benedict has always been special to my father and I know you will both make each other very happy. But when you marry and move into the vicarage, you will have to leave Benfleet Hall and I will lose you as my tutor.'

Miss Ruth is now sobbing and I too can feel tears pricking my eyes. Composing myself and suppressing my own feelings, I take a deep breath before saying anything, because I do know and fully understand her feelings and sorrow, as I felt the same when I lost my mother and had to leave Meg, Jasper and Gertie behind only three years ago. Then to lose Meg later that same year was I thought more than I could bear, but I have found the strength to cope and now can really help someone else who is hurting in a similar way.

`Dear Miss Ruth you will never lose my friendship, and I know Benedict will agree when I say that you are welcome to visit us at the vicarage whenever you need too. But you must not be afraid and let this spoil the time we have together now. Our wedding is not yet planned and I shall remain here for a while yet, I hope. As for me being your only friend, I know how much your father, Lady Elizabeth, and Mary, Sarah and Harriet are just longing to share friendship with you. The three little ones could learn so much from you, and when the time does come for me to leave, they are also going to need someone else to rely on, and you could be that person Miss Ruth, you just have to learn to trust them in the same way you do me. They all love you so much and just want you to love them back.'

By now we are both sobbing freely and I begin to doubt whether any lessons will take place this afternoon.

`Miss Isabella, do my sister's really want to be friends with me, after the way I have ignored their very existence for so long?'
My heart breaks, as I watch helplessly, this innocent child carrying the pain, burden and guilt that is weighing so heavily upon her young shoulders. I have been where she is so I must be able to help her through in the same way I was helped, but how?

`They love you Miss Ruth and all they have ever wanted is true friendship with their big sister.'
Lessons seem unimportant this afternoon, Miss Ruth needs time to talk and be completely open with someone who is not personally caught up within her life and circumstances, and I know that this is why I came to Benfleet Hall. I feel so honoured that she has chosen to trust me enough to let her real character shine out, and enable people to at last begin to get close to her. Miss Ruth and I leave the school room together this evening and only part company when we reach the door of my room. Today has been challenging in a variety of ways, not least this morning when the three younger girls found the excitement of yesterday prevented them from concentrating. This afternoon with Miss Ruth

presented a very different challenge altogether, but has been extremely rewarding for me. Feeling fulfilled and happy, I descend the stairs and join the family in the dining room for dinner.

***

Two weeks have now passed since I became engaged to Benedict, and with barely a month left before Christmas, excitement throughout the house is building. Mary, Sarah, and Harriet are much more settled in their lessons again now, and Miss Ruth has asked, if after Christmas she can join the three young ones for morning lessons. This is so encouraging for me as her tutor, but even more so for her father, Sir Abraham who had begun to doubt whether he would ever really know his oldest daughter. He certainly never expected such a dramatic change so quickly, and for her now to be building a relationship with her sisters, and Lady Elizabeth as well, he admitted to me only yesterday, is something that he could only pray for, never really expecting it to become a reality. I descend the stairs this morning with a spring in my step which developed after my engagement to Benedict, and arrive at the dining room just as Benedict appears to be leaving.

`Am I late for breakfast this morning? Or are you leaving for another reason?'

Expecting him to come out with one of his usual quick remarks, I am surprised and perturbed when his expression remains so serious.

`My dearest sweet Isabella, I heard you coming and knew I must speak to you alone, before breakfast. You are not late, and I will be joining you, but first we must talk.'

The tone of his voice and the look of horror, fear and misery on his face concerns me greatly, and I begin to feel my own anxiety and fear building.

`Dear Benedict, you are frightening me, please tell me what is wrong, where is your usual fun and light-heartedness? Have I done something to hurt or displease you?'

Taking me by the arm he gently walks me to the drawing room before speaking again.

`Isabella, how could you think such a thing? You could never displease or hurt me; none of this is your fault. What I have to say is very hard for me, and I don't want to hurt you. Please promise me you will let me finish before saying anything.'

`I promise, but what could be so bad that you can imagine that I would be hurt by it?'

I can already feel a lump in my throat and a tightening in my stomach, but the sorrow in his eyes just makes me want to hold him tightly in my arms and never let go.

`Dearest Isabella, before I tell you, you must know that my love for you is very strong and, very real and will always be so, and that whatever happens nothing will ever change that.'

Tears are beginning to prick my eyes and I am trembling all over already.

`Please believe me and try to understand that what I am doing is not because I want to leave you, but because I feel it is my duty. The war which has broken out in Crimea is not going to be over as quickly as hoped, and more troops are needed. I do not intend to fight, but I do need to serve my country, so I have enlisted as a chaplain and must leave immediately after Christmas. I would dearly love to marry you before I go, but time will not allow this to happen. I will return to you as soon as I can, and we will be married and live at the vicarage as I promised. My heart is heavy as I tell you this and prepare to leave, but please promise me you will wait, never lose hope, and most of all know and try to understand why I must do this.'

By now my tears are falling freely, and I feel as if my whole world is once again falling apart around me. But deep inside I know that he is telling me the truth, and doing what he believes to be right in the eyes of God and expected in society. Through my sobs I manage to ask a question which I know is important, and my concern for the people involved is very real.

`Have you told Sir Abraham and Lady Elizabeth yet? They need to know, but I fear they will feel as desperate as I do. You mean so much to Sir Abraham especially, and he will not want to lose you, it would destroy him.'

Holding me close and forcing a smile, he tenderly kisses my forehead.

`They know already, and it was they who told me I must tell you now, and not try to protect you by not saying anything, as this would only hurt you more when the time comes for us to part. We must not allow this to spoil the time we do have together, and at least I can spend Christmas with you before I go. Come, we both need to eat, and breakfast will wait no longer. '

Feeling numb and empty, I doubt whether I will be able to eat anything, but I allow myself to be guided back to the dining room anyway. Breakfast is a solemn and silent affair, with very little being eaten by anyone. Then Lady Elizabeth asks the girls to leave and, asks me to join her in the drawing room.

`But Lady Elizabeth, the girls' lessons begin in less than an hour, and I must prepare the room.'

`Hush, Miss Isabella, there will be no

lessons today, you need time to come to terms with what you have just heard, and I would like you to be able to rely on me for comfort in this time of such heartache and sorrow.'

With tears flowing freely again, I gratefully agree and we leave together, making our way straight to the drawing room.

The rest of today seems to pass as in a dream, nothing seems real anymore. My happiness and joy of two weeks ago has been snatched away so cruelly, and once again I feel alone and vulnerable. Benedict keeps telling me that the hope of marrying me on his return, and the knowledge that he has my heartfelt love, is the only thing that gives him courage to face what lies ahead of him. This is of little comfort to me, as I cannot get rid of the awful feeling that I may never see him again when he leaves, and how can I live then?

While I ascend the stairs to my room tonight, I fear that sleep will not come easily to me. I cannot help but imagine the horrors which await my dear Benedict on his arrival in Crimea, and can find no comfort from my own sorrow at this time. This was the first time I had ever really been looking forward to Christmas, now once again I am dreading it. But this time I don't want it to come, as I know that this brings our parting from close to imminent. The thought of being here at

Benfleet Hall without Benedict is almost too much to bear, yet at least here I can feel close to him, and I know that my duties as governess and tutor to the four girls is what is important, so here I will remain. Sir Abraham will also feel Benedict's departure deeply, and so I must console myself with the knowledge that I am still very much needed by this family, whom I have grown to love and care very deeply for.

Despite my fears of last night, I awake this morning to find that I did in fact sleep. I think I must have been exhausted with all my crying, and busying myself to take my mind off a painful and dreaded separation that is coming closer with every day that passes. My body must have needed to rest so much that nothing could prevent sleep from creeping over me like a cloud. I decide that routine is what I need most, so I get down to breakfast early with the intention of speaking to Lady Elizabeth about resuming the girls lessons this morning. But on my arrival at the dining room, the only other person already there is Benedict. My heart starts pounding and the lump in my throat returns worse than before. He has not yet noticed me as he is standing with his back towards the door, gazing longingly out of the window. My thoughts are ones of great concern and heartache for him, how can such a gentle, loving man face a cruel, loveless war? Why is he drawn to this duty so strongly? I decide to leave him to his contemplations, so I turn to leave, but before I take a single step, he speaks without turning round or even looking in my direction.

`Isabella, is that you? Please don't go, stay with me, I need you now more than ever before.'

Fighting to stay in control of my emotions, so that I do not let my own feelings and fears show. I make my way slowly across the room towards him.

`Oh Benedict, what can I say or do that can be of any help or comfort to you now?'

`You need not say or do anything, your presence here with me is enough.'

These simple words mean everything to me, yet they hurt so much. No longer in control, tears stream down my cheeks as his strong but gentle arms draw me close in an embrace, and looking up into his kind, handsome face, I notice that he too is crying.

We are still standing at the window in silent reverie when Lady Elizabeth enters the room.

`I am so glad that you two beautiful young people are able to find some comfort in each other at this time, even if it is to be so short-lived.'

Coming out of my melancholic reverie and turning quickly towards her, I have to seize this opportunity to speak with her.

`Please, Lady Elizabeth, I really must speak with you before breakfast. Excuse me Benedict, but this cannot wait.'

Releasing me from his embrace, he smiles weakly, kisses me on the head and graciously allows me to take my leave.

Following Lady Elizabeth from the dining room and into the drawing room, I take a deep breath and sit myself down before either of us speaks. Looking at me with real concern in her eyes Lady Elizabeth speaks first.

`Miss Isabella, before you ask or say what you need to, may I ask you something?'

`Of course Lady Elizabeth. What is it?'

`Well, there is more than one thing actually, the first being, did you manage to sleep at all last night?'

Surprised by the simplicity and normality of this question, I wonder what else she wants to know.

`Despite fearing that I would not sleep at all, I woke this morning having slept all night, and I do feel better today thank you.'

`That is good news, now the next question may need some thought before you give me an answer, so take your time, and while you consider it, you may like to ask or say what you wanted too. Sir Abraham and I wondered whether you may like to return to Havergal Manor when Benedict leaves, not permanently, but just for a short while so that you can be supported by your own family until you feel stronger. Now what did you want to talk to me about.'

Her second question has left me feeling completely shocked. Why does she think that being somewhere else will help? Nothing could ease the pain and sorrow which I am already feeling, and which I am certain will only increase with time. But then I suppose she is only trying to help and think of me, she probably doesn't know how to help, and thinks that I would be happier with Lady Phoebe to comfort me. I doubt whether I could find any real comfort with anyone, no matter where I am living.

`Lady Elizabeth, I thank you for your concern, but I believe that what I am about to say and ask you will answer your second question, and I trust I will need to give no other answer. It is my belief that the best way for me to cope with my heartache and sorrow is to keep a routine, and it is for this reason I am asking for your permission to recommence lessons with all four girls starting today. I also intend to continue with my duties following Benedict's departure; I am needed here and will serve you as best I can for as long as I am required. Please do not send me away, I can at least feel close to him here, even though physically we have been torn apart. If I were somewhere else that closeness could not be the same.'

Unable to speak or plead anymore, I again give way to my tears allowing them to fall freely, for what seems a long time, but in truth it is not longer than a few minutes. During this time Lady Elizabeth sits beside me holding my hand, just as Lady Phoebe had done many times before. Once I have calmed myself again, and the tears have ceased to flow for the second time this morning, Lady Elizabeth speaks again.

`Miss Isabella, of course you can recommence lessons if that is what you wish to do, and we have no intention of sending you away. You are, and have been a real blessing to this house and our family, the difference in Miss Ruth is more than we could have ever hoped for. We just don't want you to feel as if you owe us anything, or that you cannot return to Havergal Manor if you feel you need to. Sir Abraham and I were just concerned that if you stay here when Benedict departs, the memories held here may make life harder for you. But if you feel the opposite is true, then of course you can stay. I know that the girls will all be delighted. Speaking of which if you intend to begin lessons at the usual time, we should return to the dining room for some breakfast. You must eat to keep your strength up.'

Forcing a smile I reluctantly agree, and with Lady Elizabeth return to the dining room to join the rest of the family.

Although I can never forget the dreaded day of our parting, getting back into a routine with the four girls does seem to ease my torment and anguish, even if only temporarily. Christmas is now less than a week away, and despite my fervent prayers every night for the weather to deteriorate, delaying my beloved Benedict's departure, it has not happened and the snow is far less severe than in any of the years I have known previously. I am now resigned to losing him on the appointed day, and know that our long-term future and happiness may now never come to pass. The girls seem to understand my pain and are more determined than before to try to please me, doing whatever I ask of them with good grace, and always such cheery dispositions, that I even find myself smiling occasionally.

***

Today is the last day of lessons until after Christmas and New Year, so I have decided to teach the girls a Christmas carol which they will sing together, and I hope each one will also learn a poem to recite for Sir Abraham and Lady Elizabeth on Christmas Eve. This is certainly popular with Mary, Sarah and Harriet, but Miss Ruth seems uncertain and reluctant.

`Miss Ruth, are you alright? Do you not want to join in and show everyone how talented you are? I thought perhaps it would be fun, and a nice memory for Benedict to take away with him.'

`Miss Isabella, I don't mind singing with my sisters, but to do something on my own is terrifying me. Please don't make me do this, I would not know what to learn and I know I would look foolish when I stand there having forgotten the words.'

Feeling her anxiety and fear, I find that I am unsure how to give her any courage and confidence, when I have so little to draw on myself at this moment.

`Miss Ruth, no-one is going to force you to do anything, but if you feel that maybe you could write something yourself to give your cousin, I know that he would appreciate your effort.'

`Thank you Miss Isabella, I would like to do that, and if you will read something you have written I will try to do the same.'

This is not what I had expected her to say at all, and now it is my turn to panic. How can I not do what I am asking my pupils to do? But what should I read? How can I perform at a time of celebration when I feel so hopeless?

Deciding that my own struggle must be dealt with later, I suppress my feelings and begin teaching the girls Once in Royal David's City, and thinking about which poems they should learn. All four have very pretty voices, and easily learn the words and the music. By the time lessons finish, each child knows the carol and a poem which they will recite on Christmas Eve. As the three youngest girls leave the school room, excitedly skipping down the stairs, I stay behind to tidy work books and lesson plans away, assuming Miss Ruth followed her sisters out of the door. But then as I too begin to exit the room to descend the stairs, I hear a gentle humming from the small room behind the curtain, where I had first discovered Miss Ruth. I stop to listen, and gradually the humming turns to singing and appears to be getting closer. Miss Ruth then appears, and is at first unaware of my presence. As soon as she sees me however, she immediately becomes silent looking embarrassed and startled.

`Oh, Miss Isabella, I thought that everyone had already left, I only sing when I am alone.'

`But why Miss Ruth? You have a beautiful voice and were singing quite happily with the others today.'

`That is so different, because I cannot be heard then, and I would be far too shy to sing aloud if I thought that anyone was listening to me. Please don't tell father. Mother used to sing to me when I was tiny, but I fear that hearing me would hurt and upset him deeply, as his memories of her would be re-awoken.'

This unexpected revelation causes me great concern and uncertainty as I contemplate the entertainment planned for three days' time.

'But, Miss Ruth, what about the carol the four of you are performing on Christmas Eve? Do you think that will cause any distress to Sir Abraham?'

'Oh no Miss Isabella, that is quite different. He can often be heard humming or singing carols himself at Christmas time. But the song I was singing just now is one my mother used to sing, and I don't believe anyone has sung it in this house since she died, except for me that is, in private.'

'I will say nothing to anyone Miss Ruth, but you may be surprised, your father may be delighted to hear it sung again, especially so beautifully by you. He may look upon it as a tribute to your mother, some day it may provide help and comfort for him.'

'Do you really think that is possible Miss Isabella? '

'I do. But now we must go, or we will be late for dinner.'

As we descend the stairs together, I know I still have a purpose here, and even though

Benedict's departure is now only a few days away, and my heart is heavy with sorrow and concern, I have to trust and believe that he is doing the right thing.

***

Today is Christmas Eve, the decorations are up and the feast for tomorrow is being prepared. Mary, Sarah and Harriet are all full of excitement and cannot wait for this evening when they perform for the family. Miss Ruth is more subdued and obviously still nervous of performing tonight, but also seems distracted in some other way or by something else.

`Miss Ruth, are you alright? You seem quiet and solemn, are you still worried about your part in this evening's entertainment?'
Looking at her I know it is more than just nerves, and deep down I fear that she is as aware of the dangers that face her cousin on his arrival in Crimea as I am.

`I am nervous Miss Isabella, but I want to do it for Benedict. It is just that I am so frightened that when he leaves he will never come back and I know how much you love him, and he you. I am scared that you will want to leave Benfleet Hall because it holds too many memories for you, and I want to know how I can help you feel better and want to remain here with us.'
The heartfelt concern and love which this

child exudes is almost too much for me to bear, but I know that I have to try to help her stay positive, even though my own fears and feelings are almost identical to hers.

`Come now Miss Ruth, if we get upset and allow our concern and fear to show, it will make leaving here even harder for Benedict than it already is. Your father is going to feel his departure greatly too, so we must all try to stay positive and not dwell on things which may never happen.'

I hardly know why or how I am saying this myself, but an unknown, unfamiliar strength is rising up within me, enabling me to cope.

The morning and lunchtime pass uneventfully, and this afternoon while sewing in the drawing room with Lady Elizabeth, reality hits me. I am suddenly very aware that I have no poem prepared for tonight, and after Miss Ruth had promised to read something if I did, I make my excuses and hurry to my room to try and write something. I sit for a long time, but inspiration is refusing to come, and panic starts to creep over me. What can I read tonight? It has to be positive and uplifting, something that I can give to my beloved Benedict to take with him so that he always knows that back at home, there is someone who is loving him still, praying for his safe return and the time when we can be reunited, never to be parted again.

As we part and I wave goodbye,
My heart is heavy but I will not cry,
The love we share in our hearts today,
Will bring you back to my arms I pray,
Wherever you are,
Be it near or far,
My love goes with you,
With words few but true,
So united we will be,
By the wind living free.

These words flow easily on to the paper, but now I have written them so do my tears. So I sit for a while, alone in the peace of my room to regain my composure. I wake with a jolt as somebody enters my room, unaware I had drifted off to sleep.

`Miss Isabella, are you feeling unwell?' Struggling to come to my senses I gradually realise that it is Lady Elizabeth who is speaking to me and standing beside my chair.

`Oh, Lady Elizabeth, I am so sorry, please excuse me, I came up here to write a poem for tonight and must have drifted off. I am quite well thank you, and shall be down directly.'

`There is no rush Miss Isabella, I was just concerned that you had not returned to the drawing room. Take your time and come down when you are ready, dinner will be served shortly.'

Thanking her again for her concern, I hurriedly gather myself together and change for dinner.

The evening's entertainment is well received and all four girls are enchanting. Miss Ruth recites a beautiful poem that she has written specially and gives a copy to Benedict, which I can see brings him close to tears. Now it is my turn, with a lump in my throat and trembling all over I begin to read the words written that afternoon. To my utter dismay, I only manage three lines before my emotions take over getting the better of me. But it is to her credit, and everyone else's shock and surprise when Miss Ruth, seeing my distress, gets up stands beside me and reads my poem for me. I know how much courage this takes, and it could not mean more to me. To see someone who has suffered so much herself, come to my side and my aid gives me a special feeling never experienced before. It is at this point that I know I am accepted as part of this very wonderful, loving family.

Part three

It is six months ago today since I waved farewell to my beloved Benedict, and in that time I have received only one brief letter telling me that he arrived safely. I miss him so much, and with every day that passes my concern for his health and life grows more and more intense. Spring and summer here at Benfleet Hall are truly beautiful, but my heart continues to ache for him, and even my regular visits to Havergal Manor fail to ease my sorrow. The girls love doing their lessons outside, and the routine that this gives me is the only thing which gives me purpose and a focus. Will this war ever end? Can I ever hope to know the happiness I believed would be mine just a few short months ago? These questions are impossible to answer, but the one thing I do know is that I must try and remain strong and positive for Benedict's sake if not my own.

Sir Abraham is also struggling without his nephew, but is able to take great comfort and delight in the positive change in his oldest daughter. Miss Ruth is now a totally different girl from the one who I first met back in October. She is happy, relaxed and able to enjoy the company of her sisters, and although still quite timid, her self-confidence is growing by the day.

This weekend I am due to visit Havergal Manor again, but although I am glad to see Lord Sebastian, Lady Phoebe and Miss Amelia, it is my Benedict I long to be able to see and embrace again.

***

On my arrival at Havergal Manor Lady Phoebe comes out to greet me as usual, but I can see by her expression that she has something to tell me that I am not going to want to hear. I tell myself that if there were any news of Benedict, then I would have been told at Benfleet Hall before I left, but if not him then who or what could be so dreadful.

As I enter the refreshingly cool hallway, away from the intense heat of the summer sun, and proceed to the airy, bright drawing room which I know so well, a type of fear and dread which I have not experienced for a couple of years now, begins to envelope me like a heavy, dark shroud. Reality is beginning to dawn, if the news is not about Benedict, then it must relate to either my father, or worse still to Jasper or Gertie. I stop dead unable to move, and barely able to breath, a cold shiver travelling down my spine and throughout my whole body.

`Lady Phoebe you have bad news for me, please tell me what you know?'

`Come in Isabella. Please you must sit down, this is not easy to tell you, and is going to come as a huge shock to you.'

Taking my hands tightly in her own as she has done so often before, she takes a deep breath before speaking again.

`Dearest Isabella, two days ago we received word from Meg's mother Hattie that your father is dying, and that Jasper's eyesight has all but completely gone. Gertie is having to care for both of them and at just twelve years old this is too much for her to cope with. Hattie has gone back to help, leaving Agnes and Ned under the care of Miss Amelia and Miss Grace, but she cannot stay for long. It is with a heavy heart I have to ask you this question, and I know you have another heartache and concern of your own at this time, but Gertie really needs you and so does Jasper. Your father is no threat to you now, he has only days left to live, but until he dies your brother and sister refuse to leave him. Would you consider returning home until Jasper and Gertie are ready to come back here with you?'

I sit motionless and unable to speak; the true horror of this situation is all too clear. On the one hand I am needed at Benfleet Hall by four girls who I love dearly, where I am safe and as happy as I can be with Benedict in a foreign war torn country. I need to be there to be as close as I can to Benedict, and in case there is any news from or of him. On the other, my own brother and sister whom I have not seen for nearly four years, and have missed terribly need me so much more. What am I to do?

'Lady Phoebe, must I go back? I hoped and believed that I had left that life behind me, and the very thought of having to return fills me with utter dread. My father and the memories I have of my early years spent in that desolate place still terrify me, and two of my greatest fears now are, that if I return I will never again escape the evil, dishonest clutches of my father's family, and that any news of my beloved Benedict will never be made known to me.'

My fear of never seeing him again is now even more real to me, and I become faint with emotion.

'You do not have to answer now Isabella, and there is another possibility which Lord Sebastian and I can discuss with you, but now I can see you need to rest. I will help you to your room so that you may rest comfortably on the bed. Do you think you can manage the stairs if I come with you?'

'I think so, but Lady Phoebe, I do not

want to be alone, please will you stay with me? I am frightened and do not know what to do!'

Taking my arm, she slowly and gently helps me upstairs to my old room and on to the bed.

`Of course I will stay, but do try and get some rest.'

In spite of how I am feeling and the terror that is within me, the large soft bed and summer's warmth soon make it difficult for me to keep my eyes open, and how ever hard I fight it I begin to drift off to sleep.

I awake to discover the cool of evening is already upon us, and for an instant I feel relaxed and at ease. But all too quickly the memories of earlier today flood into my mind with the force of a thundering torrent, and I sit bolt upright in sheer panic and alarm.

`Isabella, you are quite safe, no-one can hurt you here, just relax and allow yourself to wake up slowly.'

But even the sweet, gently soothing voice of Lady Phoebe cannot ease my anguish, I am already wide awake and the turmoil I am feeling over the decision I have to make is enormous. The more I try and think about it, the harder it seems to get. Finally I have to give in, and tears flow freely once again.

`Oh Lady Phoebe, what am I going to do? I really don't want to go back, but if I don't I feel as though I am deserting Jasper and Gertie in their hour of need. Please help me!'

Unable to speak more, I find I am once again being comforted by Lady Phoebe as she gently and soothingly strokes my hair, in the same way she had done so often when I first arrived as a child nearly four years earlier.

`Isabella, I cannot tell you what to do, but believe me when I tell you that you will not be trapped by your old life again. You have left that life behind and nothing can take away what you have achieved, and the life you now have. Lord Sebastian and I will ensure that doesn't happen. Do you feel up to coming downstairs for a little dinner?'

`I don't think I could eat anything, but I do not want to be alone, so I will try.'

Taking hold of my arm again, Lady Phoebe supports me as we slowly make our way down to the dining room.

`Please try and eat something Isabella, you cannot face anything without the strength to do so.'

Lady Phoebe's concern for me is evident, and I know that she speaks the truth, so I manage a small amount, but every mouth full sticks in my throat and eventually I can force no more down.

***

Following a tormented and restless night, everything seems as unclear and horrible as it did yesterday. How can I possibly know what the right decision is? I cannot face any of this on my own. If only my mother and Meg were still alive, but there is no-one back at home who I can turn to now. How can I hope to help Jasper and Gertie when I cannot even help myself? I feel hopeless, despairing and alone; can nothing good ever last in my life?

A knock at my door disturbs my melancholic reverie, and Lady Phoebe enters my room.

`Isabella, I can see that you are already up and dressed, come with me down to breakfast, there is something Lord Sebastian and I need to tell you, and then discuss with you. Do you need an arm to steady you down the stairs?'

Feeling numb and at a distance from reality, I gratefully accept her arm, and we descend the stairs together.

The thought of food is still not a pleasurable one, as eating is still an effort. Breakfast is a quiet, sombre affair this morning, with nobody really knowing what to say or how to help. The weather is again hot and sunny, so when breakfast is finished we go out into the garden, but I still feel cold and shaky. This time it is Lord Sebastian who is first to speak.

`Dear Isabella, I realise the news you received on your arrival here yesterday is hard to take, and you feel pulled in all directions at the moment. Neither Lady Phoebe nor I can tell you what is the right thing to do, but we can and will support you in whatever decision you make. We also have another option for you to consider.'

My mind is so full already I doubt whether a third option is going to make my decision any easier, on the contrary I am beginning to feel even more confused than I was before. But Lord Sebastian and Lady Phoebe have done so much for me up to this point in my life; I know they will only have my best interests and welfare at heart.

`What is it Lord Sebastian?'

Lord Sebastian looks knowingly at Lady Phoebe, who again takes my hands in hers and smiles reassuringly at both myself and her husband.

`Miss Isabella, we both know and understand completely how, just the thought of returning to the home you left as a child, which holds so many fears and bad memories for you is terrifying. I own a farmhouse, which is situated about halfway between here and your father's house, and what we are proposing is that you live there with your brother and sister, and a nurse tends to your father. This means that your sister can still visit him regularly if she wishes too, but you will have the comfort of knowing this distance is between the two of you. Thomas is living there at the moment so will be available to transport whoever needs it whenever they need it. We also thought this may provide you with a feeling of some comfort and protection until you are able to return to us here, or to your duties at Benfleet Hall. We know that this is a huge decision for you and that you will have vastly conflicting emotions whatever you decide, so having spoken with Sir Abraham and Lady Elizabeth myself yesterday while you were resting, it has been decided that you should remain here with us until you have decided what you are going to do. Is that alright?'

I am so overwhelmed at the kindness and understanding everyone is showing me, I am unable to answer straight away. A few minutes pass and I manage to take in at least some of what has just been said before replying.

`I don't know what to say, or how to thank any of you. You are all so wonderful to me and at the moment I feel quite overwhelmed by your generosity and love. Please accept my thanks and will try not to take too long to make a decision, although part of me is being torn apart I already fear that I know what I must do.'

***

I remain at Havergal manor for another two days, but know in my heart that I made my decision the day after my arrival. I realised then that I could not ignore the great need of my brother and sister, and despite the cruelty my father inflicted on me as a child, I also know that as the oldest surviving child it is my duty to tend to him in his last days. As most of my belongings are still at Benfleet Hall, I take only the few things I have with me at Havergal Manor, the rest will be sent on if the need arises. Lord Sebastian and Lady Phoebe are both to accompany me on this most difficult of journeys, and I have taken up their most generous offer to stay at the farmhouse, rather than at my father's house. But before arriving there I am to visit my father, Jasper and Gertie, so I am aware of the full situation. A nurse has been employed so that Jasper and Gertie can come with me to the farmhouse when Lord Sebastian and Lady Phoebe take me on their return journey.

As I leave Havergal Manor today, my heart is heavy and fear is gripping me all over. I am numb and empty as the carriage makes its way down the long gravel drive, dapple-shaded by the trees both sides that meet above. What if my father is not really ill and this is just his latest ploy to persuade me to return home? But I know that this is most unlikely, Hattie would never be fooled, and she would certainly never tell me an untruth, forcing me to leave behind my new life, my only possible escape from a life of beatings and crime.

The journey is long and hot as we travel along unshaded roads and lanes, but pleasantly cool where trees stand like cathedral cloisters over the road. Having left Havergal Manor just after breakfast, it is nearly noon before I begin to recognise the desolate landscape through which we are now travelling. My terror builds as we get nearer to a place so hated by me, that when I left nearly four years ago I prayed that I would never again have to set my eyes on it.

Heavy grey clouds,
Hanging still and unmoving,
The atmosphere sinister,
With a darkness unyielding,
The misty moisture in the air,
Bringing dampness to a desolate scene.
The mood of this place,
As dark as the sky,
Isolation and loneliness,
Surrounding me,
Bringing fear and an anxious dread.
Uncertainty hovers,
I must escape,
But have lost my way,
And night's blackness is quickly stealing the day.

`Oh Lady Phoebe, I really don't know if I can go through with this, please will you come with me I cannot face this alone?'

My fear must show more than I realise, as it is Lord Sebastian who answers my heartfelt plea.

`Isabella, we are both going to be with you throughout today's visit. At no point will you be left alone with your father. We both believe you are showing great courage and fortitude by coming here at all, and admire you for being so loyal after all that you have been through, and sacrificed to make this journey. This decision cannot have been easy for you, and you know you will have our full support for as long as you need it.'

On our arrival at the almost derelict house, everywhere has an uncomfortable stillness and silence to it, as though a heavy cloud has enveloped this place and no person or creature has set foot here in a long while. Lord Sebastian is first to alight from the carriage, he then turns to assist Lady Phoebe and myself before knocking on the door. It is dear Hattie who answers, and beckons us quietly into the small gloomy passage before showing us through to the only bright room in the place, the kitchen! Even this is dull, cold and uninviting.

`Why, Miss Fl... err, I mean Miss Isabella I can hardly recognise you, I wasn't sure that you would even come. But I am glad you have, you may be only just in time, young Gertie has not left his side for three days, and is desperately in need of reassurance and rest. The nurse arrived yesterday, but still your sister will not leave him. Dear Miss Isabella, would you follow me and I will take you straight to your father's room.'

`Oh Hattie, thank you for all that you have done, but I know where to go and Lady Phoebe is coming with me. I need her support to do this, please try to understand. '

`Of course I understand, please try and persuade Gertie to take some rest.'

`Jasper and Gertie will be leaving with me today; we are going to be staying at a farmhouse just a few miles away, they both need to get away.'

Holding on to Lady Phoebe's arm we make our way to my father's room, stopping outside to take a few deep breaths, I push the door gently, and we enter. Gertie has grown so much I barely recognise her, but she must recognise me as she instantly jumps up and runs into my arms. For several minutes we cling tightly to each other, unable to move or speak.

`Flora, you've come back, I never thought I would see you again, why did you leave us? Why did you never send for us?'

My heart is aching with regret and sorrow, but still I know I did the right thing. There would have been no escape or hope for any of us if I had not left when I did.

'Oh Gertie please do not blame Isabella, we tried to bring you and Jasper to be with your sister, but your father was so angry about her leaving, he refused to let you come. But soon dear child you will all be able to escape from here forever, come to Havergal Manor and live the life you deserve. Until then you will all be together a few miles from here in a farmhouse that we own where you will be safe, but still able to visit your father daily if that is what you want.'

'Who are you? What are you doing here?'
Shocked and a little embarrassed by Gertie's outburst and lack of manners, I almost turn and run out of the room and the house, but Lady Phoebe's grip tightens and soothingly she pats my hand.

'Gertie! Mind your manners, this is Lady Phoebe, and it is she and her husband Lord Sebastian who have very generously ensured that you and Jasper have been provided for since I left. Just you apologise this minute!'

Looking at Gertie's face I know instantly that I have been too harsh on her and immediately go to comfort her. But it is Lady

Phoebe who takes Gertie in her arms, and encourages me to go over to my father's bed. Looking at him I cannot believe that this thin, frail, old looking man, is the same man who inflicted such cruelty on me, my fear begins to melt into pity as I take his skeletal hand in mine, and bend to kiss his pale, shallow cheek. Tears brim over, how could I ever have doubted that coming here was the right thing to do? This once proud, bully of a man is no threat to anyone now, he is the one who is alone and frightened, I can help and provide comfort to him even though he could never do the same for me.

It is mid-afternoon before Lord Sebastian, Lady Phoebe, Jasper, Gertie and I emerge from my father's house, leaving the nurse and Hattie to care for him. Dear, sweet Hattie has most kindly agreed to stay until he dies, so that Jasper and Gertie would come with me for a well-earned rest, and to give us all a chance to get to know each other again. All five of us now climb up into the carriage, and make our way back along the road to the farmhouse.

The shadows are beginning to lengthen as the sun starts to lose height in the early mid-summer evening, but this just means the journey is cooler and less uncomfortable than earlier. It is nearly time for dinner before we reach our destination, and Lord Sebastian and

Lady Phoebe have at least another two hours of travelling ahead of them, when they leave here. But as always they assure me that Jasper, Gertie and I are the priority today, so will remain with us until we are settled. Thomas is not around when we arrive, but unbeknown to me our meal has already been provided and is waiting for us on our arrival.

Surrounded by trees, nestled in the foot hills, stands the white painted farmhouse that is to be our new home at least for a while. Its setting was certainly dramatic, but somehow the house appears lonely and sad, reflecting my own feelings. We enter through the front door and my heart sinks yet further, the hallway is narrow and dark with no heating. How can I find any comfort or be inspired to write anything in a place like this? But even this place is better than living with my father again, and it is a very generous offering so we will make the best of it and enjoy being together again.

The large kitchen is light and airy and looks out onto a pretty garden and the hillside beyond; this is better but everywhere feels so cold and unloved in spite of the summer heat outside. The lounge has a huge open fire place, so I set to work making a fire. Once lit, life seems to return to the house, albeit slowly and the chilly dampness begins to fade. The bedrooms are light but small and the furniture seems tired, but at least we can call this our own, until we are able to return to Havergal Manor, and hopefully in time I will be able to resume my duties at Benfleet Hall.

***

A few weeks pass, and something in me is changing. I no longer hate this house; in fact I am beginning to want to know its history. This is however proving to be quite difficult because no-one I meet appears to want to talk about it; even Thomas appears unwilling to help me unravel the truth. This seems strange to me, but only goes to add to the intrigue making me more determined to find out about our current home.

***

Weeks become months and still father clings to life, defying all expectations. I find myself creating a history for `Foothills Farmhouse' to help me pass the time and keep my mind away from Benedict, as I have still heard nothing from him or any news of him. From this point on Lord Sebastian's farmhouse proves to be a truly inspiring place although I still long for the time we are able to make the journey back to Havergal Manor and leave this life behind us for good. But winter is now creeping towards us again, and the journey is far too hazardous to undertake in bad weather, so unless father gives up the fight soon, we will be trapped here until spring. Thankfully the rest of my belongings arrived from Benfleet Hall a few days ago, so I have warmer clothes to put on. Lord Sebastian and Lady Phoebe have also sent warm clothes for both Jasper and Gertie, so we have all we need to spend the winter here, but the desolate landscape and isolation of this place are filling me with dread again. I am now more certain than ever that this place holds a sinister secret of its own, and the feeling that it is somehow connected to my family continues to increase and strengthen with every passing day.

***

Today is the fifteenth day of November, and although last week saw the first real snow of winter, this morning has a cold crispness to it, and a weak winter sun hangs low in sky bringing an eerie glow to the mist swirling round my feet in this desolate, austere, bleak, sinister landscape. Thomas has been, and is such a support to all of us, especially Jasper who seems to really relate to him, talking to him as I never thought Jasper would talk to anyone. Nothing is too much trouble, but I cannot shake the feeling that he is hiding something from me, from us. Still, he is such a gentleman that I feel sure it is for our protection, rather than for any less honourable reason.

As I turn from gazing out of the back door,

entering the kitchen to clear the breakfast table and begin to make preparation for lunch, Gertie runs into the kitchen with tears streaming down her cheeks.

`Oh Gertie, you startled me, whatever is the matter? Is it Jasper? Sit down child, take a deep breath and tell me what has happened to distress you so.'

Drying my hands, I move away from the sink and take a seat beside the quivering form of my young sister. Wrapping a blanket around her shoulders, I draw her onto my lap and into my arms, something I have not done since she was a much younger child, and yet it feels so natural.

`Oh Flora, I mean Isabella, Hattie is on her way here from our house, I can see her in the distance, and she has borrowed a pony and trap so it must mean father. Something has happened, and not one of us was with him, I should never have left his side.'

Seeing the terror and anguish in Gertie's face I know just what she is feeling. Just four and half years earlier, this had been me when our mother died. Trying not to let my own feelings show, I endeavour to comfort and calm her, but with little success.

`Hush now Gertie, we don't know anything for sure, so we must wait until Hattie arrives before deciding what to do, or blaming ourselves for something which we could have no influence over. We all know how sick father is, and that it is only his stubbornness that has seen him last this long. If the end has come, then we must believe that he is now at peace and that this is right for him and us.'

The sudden and desperate knock at the back door heralds Hattie's arrival, and the news we have all been expecting. Father has taken a dramatic turn for the worse over night, and Hattie came as soon as it was light to tell us personally.

`Please come with me now Miss Isabella, bring Gertie and Jasper too. I have grave doubts whether we will be in time, but I did tell the nurse I would try to get you there.'

`We are ready Hattie, Gertie saw you from a long way off and is already convinced that it is her fault, because she did not remain with him constantly. Jasper is very solemn and quiet as usual, but I think he knows what is to come too.'

`I am sure he does Miss Isabella, his eyes may be weak, but he has as much knowledge as you or I. I'm afraid it is going to be a cold journey for you all, but at least it is dry and the snows of winter have not yet set in, so the journey is not too perilous.'

`Dear Hattie, thank you so much for all you have done for us, we are never going to be able to pay such a debt of gratitude as we owe you.'

`Nonsense, you owe me nothing! If it weren't for you, Agnes, Ned and I would be in the workhouse or worse. It is only thanks to you that we have a house to live in, food on the table and clothes on our backs. If you hadn't escaped and been living the life dear Martha wanted for you, my dear Meg would have been murdered for sure, instead of being able to die in comfort with her dearest friend by her side. We would have nothing, so it is we who owe you, not you us, so we'll have no more talk like that!'

`Thank you Hattie, that means so much. I will never forget the special and most precious of friendships I shared with Meg. She was the only person I could talk with who would understand.'

`I know that, and I know that you would have done the same for her if circumstances were different. Now let's have no more talk like this, there is enough sorrow to come for the three of you without dwelling on what has gone before.'

`You are right Hattie, but with hope of a better future for all of us, we will find the strength to cope.'

The rest of our journey passes in near silence, and although bitingly cold in the wind, it is the dread of what we are about to face which chills me to the bone. I have sent word with Thomas to Havergal Manor before we left the farmhouse, as I had been instructed to do by Lord Sebastian back in the summer, when I had first arrived back at this place. The knowledge that I will soon return to Havergal Manor is the only light that I can see in the darkness that now seems to hover over us like a cloud, just waiting to envelop us within its huge black cloak. Our destination can now be clearly seen, and is getting nearer with every gallop the pony takes. I can feel my heart thumping, and Gertie is huddled in the blanket with her head buried in my lap still sobbing intensely. This time I have to be strong enough to support Jasper and Gertie through their grief, and not let mine overtake me as it has done before. As we draw to a halt outside my father's house, I am aware that the feeling of guilt I have this time, is not one of not being there for him, but one of relief that finally my years of torment and fear are drawing to a close. At least from this particular source, what lies ahead I cannot see or know, but my father can no longer be a threat or danger to me or Jasper and Gertie, and for this I can only be thankful.

On our arrival at the house, I am relieved for Gertie's sake that we have made it in time. As we enter father's room his breathing is shallow and laboured, and it is obvious that the time has come. Jasper and Hattie decide to remain outside the room. Jasper says that he wants to remember him as he was, not as he is now, and the gloominess of the bedroom makes it even harder for him to see. Hattie feels that she would be intruding on what is a private family time, so says she will look after Jasper. Gertie wants me to stay with her, so we take our seats beside his bed, Gertie holding his now limp, white skeletonic hand, and me holding and attempting to console Gertie. We do not have to wait long, as within an hour of our arrival it is all over and father is at rest.

Today my father we say goodbye,
And my years of torment and fear,
Have died and gone with you,
I have been set free,
To live and be loved,
Yet an ache in my heart remains unfilled,
As my father I loved you,
Whatever I suffered,
I felt your pain, your anguish, your hate,
But did you ever really love me at all?
This is a question which will forever remain,
Unanswered and an unknown mystery to
me.

***

Today is our father's funeral, and as we leave this gloomy ramshackle dwelling for what I pray is the last time, having collected the few possessions which mean anything to us that were remaining here, Jasper, Gertie and myself are really able to begin our new lives together from today. Thomas returned from Havergal Manor the day of Father's death, with the news that they are awaiting our arrival immediately after the funeral has taken place. Lord Sebastian has most generously sent the carriage to take us to the funeral and from there directly to Havergal Manor. Our luggage is packed and loaded onto the carriage and we embark with very mixed emotions, but also a very real sense of hope.

The funeral is brief but poignant, and soon we are making the journey away from hopelessness, loneliness and desolation, towards hope, safety, security, love and friendship. This is a journey I never thought would happen for Jasper and Gertie, and when I had to return, my future seemed to be slipping away again too. But at last we can be reunited properly and live the life which our dear mother so longed to be able to give us, and was never able to.

The hope and peace I felt this morning, knowing I was returning to a place I love gave me strength to cope with a hard and painful funeral. But now as Havergal Manor is getting closer, an uneasy, anxious feeling is rising up within me, something is wrong, and

I fear the news that is to greet me relates to Benedict. I cannot bear to think of him so far from home and those he loves, and who love him, I know in my heart something is very wrong. Try as I might, I cannot shake the feeling that I will never see him again. Looking across the carriage at Jasper and Gertie, both sleeping soundly after the emotion of this morning, I too close my eyes, not to sleep, but to hide the tears that are fighting to escape.

We arrive at Havergal Manor just as daylight is beginning to fade. Feeling cold, numb and empty, we are glad and relieved to be welcomed into the warm bright drawing room and finally be able to feel safe. Jasper and Gertie seem to revive almost immediately, the look of wonder displayed in their faces as they try to take in their new surroundings bringing me some comfort and pleasure, but the dread of more bad news is still building inside me.

Lady Phoebe enters almost immediately; she is accompanied by Miss Grace and Miss Amelia.

`Miss Isabella, I have missed you so much, please say you will stay, at least until after Christmas, I could not bear for you to leave again so soon.'

`Now Miss Amelia, Isabella is tired and needs time to recover without your incessant babbling. But after a hot meal and a good night's sleep, I am sure she will have time and energy to spend with you, and want to renew your friendship.'

At this Miss Amelia turns to leave the room, but before she reaches the door, Lady Phoebe speaks again.

`Miss Amelia, this is Isabella's brother and sister, could you go with Miss Grace and take them to see their rooms, I need to speak with Isabella alone.'

`Lady Phoebe, what is it? I have had the feeling all the way back here today that something is wrong, please tell me, is it about my dearest Benedict?'

Now I am being wrapped in an embrace of love, and made to feel as safe as I had when I first arrived as child just over four years earlier.

`Dearest Isabella, we received word from Benfleet Hall that a letter had arrived addressed to you. It was brought here this morning, but as Sir Abraham also received one, I fear I already know what is contained within it.'

A shiver runs down my spine as Lady Phoebe hands me a small cream envelope, addressed to Miss Isabella Havergal, Benfleet Hall. It had been sent inside the letter addressed to Sir Abraham. I know at once that it is my Benedict's handwriting, and a glimmer of hope appears on the horizon. Trembling I open the envelope, unfold the letter and begin to read. That glimmer of hope is soon dashed and I feel as if my whole world is crashing down around me, as I read the following.

Dearest Sweet Isabella,

It is with much sorrow and regret that I tell you if you are reading these lines, it is because I have succumbed to the fever that is rife in these parts. It breaks my heart to know I can never give you the life we had planned, but please believe me when I say, it is only my love for you and yours for me, that gave me the courage I needed to face this, my final journey. Promise me you will live for both of us and not regret a minute that we spent together. My final prayer is that you will meet someone who can give you that which I have not been able too, and you must never feel guilty about giving your most precious gift of love to another who makes you feel special and secure. Your future happiness is what I long for.

Farewell my love, but not goodbye,
Eternally yours,
Benedict.

I sit unable to move or speak for several

minutes, I am not even able to cry, and I just feel numb, empty and cold. The sorrow and despair which are enveloping me right now is so much more than I have ever experienced before.

`What am I going to do? Lady Phoebe, my whole life has been turned upside down, my future and happiness snatched away by a war in a country unknown to me. I won't even have a grave I can visit, this is too cruel, will I never know happiness and joy that will last. The love we shared was precious, unique between us, how can I ever feel that way with someone else. Oh Lady Phoebe, will this pain ever end?'

Unable to continue, tears finally begin to fall, and I curl up with my head resting in Lady Phoebe's lap just as I had done so often before, and just as Gertie had done with me only days earlier.

`Isabella, I cannot answer all your questions or take your pain away, and I can only imagine how you are feeling at this moment. But what I can do is provide comfort and support for you as long as is necessary, and assure you that you will remain here until you decide what you want to do. Sir Abraham and Lady Elizabeth would welcome your return at Benfleet Hall if you decide that is what you want, but are very willing for you to visit anytime if you feel that would help you. The pain you feel now will ease in time as it has in the past, you should know this more than I, and joy and happiness can and will be yours again. You will never forget Benedict and the love you shared with him, and it would not be right if you did. But I am sure he would want you to be loved and to love again, so take life a day at a time and allow yourself to grieve, but do not feel guilty when you find yourself looking forward and enjoying life again. There will still be dark days, but they will get fewer and the bright, happy ones will gradually begin to increase. You must allow yourself time and space and not try to force things to happen quicker or slower than they are. Now hush child and just let it out.'

Without saying a word I hand Lady Phoebe the letter so that she can see, that what she has just said is reflected so closely in the words that Benedict himself has written.

`Isabella, this letter was addressed to you, its contents are therefore meant only for your eyes.'

`Please Lady Phoebe, I want you to read it, part of what you have just said to me, without knowing the letters content, has reinforced almost word for word that which Benedict has conveyed. It would mean so much for you to know the content of this letter, and therefore understand when I want to talk about how I am feeling. You would be helping me by fulfilling this request I am making.'

`Alright Isabella, if you would like someone else to read it and know its content, then I would be honoured to be this person. '
As Lady Phoebe reads through the letter, I can see that she too is deeply moved by the sentiment expressed and the words used.

`Thank you Isabella, for sharing such a heartfelt and personal letter with me, and I am so glad that Benedict has said how much he wants you to move on and be happy. You must now believe, and know in your heart that he wants you to be able to share your life and love with someone special, who thinks as much of you and makes you as happy as he did himself.'

`Oh Lady Phoebe, I doubt whether I will ever feel that way again, how could I? It would feel as though I was being disloyal to him, and yet the thought of not sharing my life with someone fills me with such fear. I do not want to be alone forever but Benedict was so special and to lose him like this is horrible. I will be so afraid of losing another special person in a similar way, and I don't think my heart could take this twice.'

`Hush Isabella, that is highly unlikely to happen, just remember how special he made you feel and how much you meant to him. Then think whether it is fair to yourself, someone else or Benedict's memory to deny that privilege and honour of re-awakening the joy and happiness that real unity with someone can bring to everyone's lives.

Let me assist you to your room so you can rest, and then you can collect Jasper and Gertie from their rooms and bring them down to the dining room in time for dinner. You must eat something so that you have the strength to help your brother and sister settle in and adapt to their new life. This is going to be a huge change for them, and although they appear excited now, I am certain that you will remember how you felt when you first arrived. They need you and you need them, so that you can all support and look after each other. You are the only person they know here, and the only family they have left. We will support you so that you can support them.'

`That means everything to me Lady Phoebe, thank you so much, your generosity, love and kindness are quite overwhelming.'

I wake to discover that night has already spread her velvet cloak of darkness across the sky, and snow is falling outside my window covering the ground with a shimmering blanket of white. Winter has arrived and so have we, we made it home before Christmas, only just in time. Although today has been painful, hard and filled with such great sorrow, just the reassurance of being back here, where we are safe and secure is already beginning to give me a little comfort.

***

We have already been back at Havergal Manor for two weeks. Jasper is now known as Master Bartholomew and Gertie as Miss Louisa. It is important that we all adopt new identities, as our father's parents are still living and pose a very real threat to us and our future as they could decide to try to trace our whereabouts. We are now the only surviving heirs to their estate, so whatever has gone before family honour is at stake and we are still in line to inherit. These new identities will not necessarily prevent us from being found, but it is hoped that it will delay their search, therefore giving us slightly greater protection and possibly even a little warning.

Bartholomew and Louisa are settling in well, although are unimpressed when Miss Grace is introduced as their tutor. They feel that education should be a choice and that having lessons every day is very unfair. This causes everyone else mild amusement, but I know that they will eventually adapt to this routine and begin to enjoy learning and achieving new things. In spite of their feelings about regular lessons, Miss Grace is already a firm favourite with Miss Louisa.

Lessons are hard and a struggle for Master Bartholomew because of his poor eyesight, but Lord Sebastian has already arranged for the provision of spectacles thus improving his life and his enjoyment of learning. Although apprehensive, Master Bartholomew is quite excited by this and looking forward to the possibility of being able to see clearly again.

The loss of my dear sweet Benedict has left a void that, at the present time feels as though it will never be filled. With Christmas once again on the horizon, in fact in only about three weeks' time, it is now I feel my loss most deeply. In only one months' time it will be a year since I waved my Benedict off, as he left to serve his country, and as he saw it, do his duty. Now all I have is memories of that day to remember him by, apart from a few short weeks prior to his departure, during which we were able to spend time together. He made me so happy and, now as I look back, extremely proud when I think about how smart he had looked in his uniform. Christmas has never been a happy time for me, and once again I am dreading it. The one bright light in the midst of my melancholic despondency is that for the first time since our dear mother died, the three of us will be together, and Bartholomew and Louisa will finally experience a proper Christmas celebration. Oh how I have longed for this to come true for them and me, but my joy may never be complete.

***

The festive preparations are well underway, and in spite of myself, some enjoyment is to be found in watching how much fun and joy is being expressed by my brother and sister. To see them safe and happy is such a comfort, and I know that mother would be so pleased to think that finally we can all enjoy the life that she so longed to be able to provide for us.

I have spoken to Lady Phoebe at length about my future, and have decided that come the spring I shall return to Benfleet Hall and recommence my duties as governess and tutor. I have missed the girls greatly and the daily routine of lessons and supporting the girls is exactly what I need. I have yet to tell Bartholomew and Louisa, but this can wait until after Christmas. There is very little point in worrying and upsetting them now, as I will be unable to leave until the weather breaks anyway. So I intend to spend as much time with them and Miss Amelia as I can over the rest of the winter, Miss Amelia's friendship and support since my return here has been amazing. She and Louisa have also become extremely close and as her brother and sister have turned their backs on her so will not be coming here at all, she sees Bartholomew and

Louisa as her siblings too. I am hoping that this will make my departure in spring less traumatic for all three of them.

***

Hattie returned to the lodge before father's funeral, so was not able to attend, but I think this would have been too painful for her, as it was through loyalty to my father Silas, that Hattie's husband Seth was hanged. Ned and Agnes were so excited when they heard that Jasper and Gertie, (now Bartholomew and Louisa) were coming to live at Havergal Manor, that Lord Sebastian and Lady Phoebe are making arrangements for them to come here in the spring, so that they can all have their lessons together. This will be easier for Miss Grace and also for Miss Amelia who is now assisting with teaching the children. It also means that the children can learn from each other.

***

Today is Christmas Eve and Thomas has also made it home for the festivities, although his journey from the farm has been hard, long and at times in his own words, `more than perilous.' We are all able to be together in safety to celebrate this year, I just wish the tragedies that have befallen me had not occurred, and that absent friends were able to be with us, instead of being parted from us so cruelly. The hopes and dreams I had for next year are now not going to happen, and the future is again looking hollow and empty. The leaden grey skies outside my window are doing nothing to lift my mood.

As another year draws to its close,
And I say goodbye to all its woes,
I look to a new one,
That seems empty and hollow,
With dreams that are shattered,
And hopes that are dashed,
I cannot forget,
The pain and the loss,
That has bruised me,
And left me bereft.
The love of my heart,
Was torn away,
By a war so distant and cruel,
We buried my father,
And with him my fear,
But for him I still shed a tear.
I long to be happy,
To love and be loved,
By a man I can no longer have.
So facing a future,
So different than planned,
I pray for courage,
And the strength to fight on.

***

Although Christmas is now almost three

months ago, today being the fifteenth day of March, the icy grip of winter seems unwilling to lessen its stranglehold on the weather. This winter is longer and harsher than I have known before, and still there is no sign of spring's arrival. This also means my return to Benfleet Hall has been delayed more than once. Thomas also has not yet been able to return to the farmhouse, but has been quite happy to remain here. Both Lord Sebastian and Lady Phoebe are more than a little surprised by their son's attitude at having to stay longer, but he seems particularly content when he is able to catch me alone. He is certainly pleasant company, but as time goes on I am beginning to feel slightly ill at ease when I am alone with him for more than a few minutes. I am beginning to suspect that he wants more than friendship from me, and although he is very dear to me I know I could never think of him in that way. This afternoon I, once again, find myself his only companion.

`Miss Isabella, I do so enjoy these afternoons we spend together, when we can talk and be alone as adults for a while. It is at these times I find myself wishing that winter would last forever, so I would never have to return to the farmhouse.'

`Why Master Thomas? What can you find so fascinating about me and the things I talk about? I can understand why you would not wish to return to the farmhouse, I never felt quite safe there myself, although that is no reflection on you. You were the perfect host and a gentleman at all times as well as such a support to us all, especially Bartholomew. I had never seen him enjoying life and communicating with anyone so much as I did in those five long months. But I really do hope that winter's grip will be broken soon, my desire to return to Benfleet Hall, and my duties there is growing by the day.'

`But why this overwhelming desire to leave Miss Isabella? Do you not enjoy my company? Are you not fond of me?'
This was the question I had been expecting for some time now, but dreading all the same. How do I respond? What should I say? What is he expecting of me? Stumbling slightly for words, I attempt to make him aware of my feelings firmly, but not unkindly.

`Master Thomas, you are a very dear friend to me, and have been since well before my arrival here. After all it was you who first bought me the news which began to restore my hope of escaping my old life. But I'm afraid I never have nor ever could think of you in any other way. You are like my lovely older brother who has always been by my side in a crisis, I really do not wish to hurt or upset you, but you must understand that anything more than friendship would only spoil the love which we have for one another.'

I can see by the expression which is creeping over his face, that this is not the response he had either wanted or expected.

`I see. I fear I may have presumed too much from our afternoons together, I am sincerely sorry if I have caused you any offence.'

The hurt in his voice is palpable, and I feel a lump come into my throat, so am greatly relieved when the door to the drawing room opens, and Miss Amelia enters with Miss Louisa close behind her.

`Isabella, Miss Amelia has been telling me the story of how she was able to creep into your room in the middle of the night. Please can you show me the secret door and passage way?'

Feeling concerned about exactly how much Miss Amelia has told my young sister, I decide that it is probably just as well that she knows about it now, so that if an occasion should arise for her to need an escape route, she would have one. Although the very thought of this need ever arising fills me with fear, as it could only mean one thing. Our father's parents had discovered our whereabouts.

`Amelia, I really wish you had spoken to me first, but if you really want to see it

Louisa, I will take you now. Where is Bartholomew? He had better come too; otherwise I will only have to repeat the tour another time.'

`He is in his room Isabella.'

`Well we can collect him on our way then. Follow me.'

I am actually quite relieved that I have been given a reason to leave Thomas's company this afternoon. I begin to feel that his hurt is coupled with some other emotion resembling either resentment or jealousy of my poor Benedict. This is causing me to feel hurt and angry at him, and I do not want to feel this way. This escape is timed perfectly, although now anxiety of another kind is building within me. If we are ever traced and found by our grandparents, our very lives could once again be in great danger. Why am I even beginning to think like this again? Thoughts like these have not entered my thinking for years. Or have they? Why was I so uncomfortable and uncertain while living with Thomas at the farmhouse? What secret was he keeping from me? Knowing I need answers to my questions, and reasons for the feeling of anxious fear now welling up inside me, I decide I must speak with Lady Phoebe today. I need to know more about father's family, and what hold they may or may not have over us.

Both Bartholomew and Louisa are fascinated by the secret passage linking my room with that of Miss Amelia, and they decide that this would be a great start to an unknown adventure. This being the case I suggest that they go and spend the rest of the afternoon writing a story about it, so that they can show Miss Grace tomorrow morning. This idea seems to meet with the approval of both of them, which in itself is nothing short of miraculous, as usually they never agree on anything, especially if I suggest it.

On my return to the drawing room, I discover that Thomas has left and Lady Phoebe has taken up her position beside the large fire that is glowing enticingly and filling the room with warmth which is felt as soon as you open the door to enter.

`Excuse me Lady Phoebe, may I speak with you? Fear and anxiety are once again growing within me, I hope that you will be able to allay my fears, and give me at least some of the answers I seek.'

`Of course Isabella, you know I am always here for you and your family, what is it that is troubling you so? I hope it is nothing which has happened here since your return that is causing you to feel this way. Please, come and sit beside me. We will not be disturbed.'

I am slightly taken aback by her last

statement, could Master Thomas have said something to her? Or does she suspect something anyway? Do I mention how I feel and what happened earlier this afternoon or not? My concern and uneasiness must show more than I am aware of, as it is Lady Phoebe who speaks again.

`What is it Isabella? You are very ill at ease this afternoon, and this is unlike you. I have not seen you like this for a long time.'
I decide to start by explaining about Thomas, and then pursue my main concern afterwards.

`Oh Lady Phoebe, please don't think me foolish but over the last few days I have begun to feel less than comfortable when alone with Thomas. Then this afternoon my concerns were confirmed, he wants more than friendship with me, and I fear he is jealous of what Benedict and I shared albeit briefly. I am sorry but I do not feel able to respond to his desire, and although I tried to explain my feelings to him earlier, I fear that I may have hurt him, and that he now not only resents Benedict but me also.'

`My dear Isabella, Thomas has always had feelings for you, so when you and Benedict became engaged he felt that his chance of happiness with you was lost. This is why he moved to the farmhouse and was so delighted when you agreed to stay there when your father was dying. Lord Sebastian and I have both spoken at length with him, and explained that he must not put any pressure on you as you are still grieving for Benedict and your father. What he said this afternoon was unfair of him and I will speak to Lord Sebastian about it. Of course you cannot force feelings which do not naturally exist, and Thomas will have to learn to accept and understand this. Do not worry yourself about this anymore, there really is no need.'

It is a great relief to me to hear these words, but my biggest concerns are far less easy for me to put into words.

`Thank you Lady Phoebe, that is very reassuring, I have always looked on Thomas as my lovely older brother, so I am afraid that anything more than friendship would spoil the special love that I hold for him.'

`Of course it would, so be secure in the knowledge that there will be no repeat of this afternoon.

Now, I think know I you well enough Isabella to be sure that there is something else of far greater concern to you than Thomas, and I fear I may already have an idea of what it is, so please continue. There are certain things I need to tell you, but I need to make sure that your concerns are the same ones that I have answers too. '

Hearing this, my heart begins to pound even harder, is my fear and anxiety justified after all? Are we once again at risk or in danger? Will we never be able to escape this life of living under the shadow created by father's trade?

`Lady Phoebe, while we were staying at the farmhouse, I could never feel completely comfortable or secure, and I continuously thought that Thomas was keeping something from me, as though he was protecting us from something or someone. I need to know about father's family, and whether or not they still have some kind of hold over us. I also need to know how much of a danger they are to us. I am scared Lady Phoebe, not just for me, but for Bartholomew and Louisa as well. Please tell me what you know, and how I can protect what remains of my family.'

Seeing the concern in Lady Phoebe's face does nothing to relieve my own fear, but I know I must hear what she has to say however unsettling and concerning it is.

`Isabella, what I am about to tell you is for your ears alone, Bartholomew and Louisa must not find out unless absolutely necessary, they are to young and vulnerable to be able to fully absorb and understand the gravity of what I am about to say. Can you remember when I told you that Miss Amelia was the daughter of Lord Sebastian's brother, that her mother had died in childbirth, and that her stepmother was cruel to her especially after her own two children were born? '

`I do, but what has that got to do with me and my father's parents? Lord Sebastian is my mother's cousin; he cannot be related to father as well can he?'

Taking hold of my hands in hers, Lady Phoebe continues her story.

`No he is not related to Silas, but his sister-in-law, Amelia's stepmother is Silas's younger sister.'

A cold shiver runs through me, as though ice is running through my veins.

`So what does this mean? I did not even know father had a sister.'

`She was only a child when your father married your mother and when Nettie, and later you were born. Because your father was the male child, it was he, and on his death your brother who were the rightful heirs to your grandparents estate. But when your father refused to let his parents take your brother to live with them, and be bought up in a suitable way as befitting a future Lord of the Manor, your family were cut off without a penny. This meant that any male child born to your father's sister would inherit everything unless your father died. Then as the oldest surviving male heir your brother would automatically take this position as soon as he reached the age of twenty-one. Obviously your aunt, Silas's sister, does not want her son to lose his inheritance, so it is she who poses the greatest risk, and Bartholomew's very life will be her target. Your grandparents are still living, and unfortunately their target is also your brother, but for a very different reason. They still want him to inherit the family estate, but this would mean you and Louisa being parted from him permanently while he is educated in the duties and responsibilities which will one day be his, as he takes his place as Lord of the Manor. This is not an inheritance which would be of any benefit to either Bartholomew or you two girls. Your grandparents are involved with the smuggling trade just as your father Silas was, but they are the top of the chain, not as your father was, risking his life, and that of his fellow smugglers, as well as the lives of his entire family. They are the people who purchase and sell the goods, not spend every night collecting, transporting and hiding them from the authorities. Unfortunately Lord Sebastian's brother also plays a role in this unlawful, dark occupation, and is not a kind man.

Your grandparents still hold the misguided idea that you children owe them a debt of gratitude for the `kindness' shown to your mother and grandmother all those years ago. This is not true Isabella, so never feel guilty about something which you had no knowledge of until you first arrived here, and certainly cannot influence or be held responsible for history. Your grandparents may well try to find you, unfortunately your aunt may already know you are here, and she would certainly not delay in betraying you to them. So when the weather does begin to improve, we must all be very aware, and vigilant. If you see or hear anything that is unfamiliar to you, or makes you feel uncomfortable, you must report it directly to either Lord Sebastian or myself. '

All this news about family I never knew existed, and the hatred they appear to have for us is worse than I had feared.

`Oh Lady Phoebe, is our very presence here at Havergal Manor not endangering the lives of anyone who lives here? I cannot bear to think that tragedy and misfortune should strike anyone else here because of us; I would never be able to forgive myself. '

Tears, guilt and panic are now consuming me like never before, and still I have no knowledge of where these relatives live, or why the farmhouse never felt safe.

`Now Isabella, you and your family are important to Lord Sebastian and myself, so any risks we take, or danger we find ourselves in, is of our own choosing. You and your brother and sister are most welcome here and are certainly in no way to blame for any of this, do you understand? '

Unable to speak, I nod my head gratefully accepting the gentle arm round my shoulders and the ability to be able rest my head on hers.

`Are you alright if I continue? There is not much more to tell, but you do need to hear it.'

`Please, I must know, so do continue, I would rather hear it all.'

`Alright, but you must believe me when I say that you are very special to us and we would never blame you, Bartholomew or Louisa for anything which may or may not happen. This last part is going to be the hardest for you to hear and cope with, but in some ways it is the most important. The farmhouse is the property of whoever is living here at Havergal Manor, but Lord Sebastian's brother is very resentful of this, insisting that as it is closer to the property he owns it should belong to him. In order to punish Lord Sebastian for refusing to give it to him, he often uses it to store his contraband, knowing that in the eyes of the authorities, Lord Sebastian would be seen to be just as guilty as he is because it is his property and he is aware of what is going on there. He, your aunt and your grandparents are all working together in this, so while you were staying at the farmhouse Thomas had to prevent them from coming. He did this willingly but you will certainly never be safe to return there. Your grandparent's estate is not far from there, and when your father died, Thomas did not notify them until you were all safely back here, and all with your new names and identities. He is known to them by a different name, and as far as we know they do not associate him with you or us.'

`But that means that Thomas must be working for them. Oh Lady Phoebe, he must stop before he gets caught, or... oh it is just too horrible to think of.'

`Hush now Isabella, Thomas is not smuggling for anyone, he lives there as farm manager, under a different name as I said earlier. All he does for any of them is carry messages, the content of which he is very careful never to discover. If he ever came to be in any danger from the authorities he would very quickly name the real culprits. `

`Please Lady Phoebe, where do my aunt and grandparents live?'

`Isabella, please believe me when I tell you that it is safer for all of you if that information is not known to you.'

`Will you at least tell me whether they live together or separately?'

`Very well, because Lord Sebastian is the oldest brother, it was he that inherited the title, and with it Havergal Manor, The Lodge that Hattie and her children now occupy and the farmhouse. This meant that Obadiah, Lord Sebastian's younger brother, was left with `The Croft`, a small property on the edge of the fells. He lived there until Amelia's mother died and he remarried, when he moved into your grandparent's property only a few miles from the farmhouse and your father's own humble dwelling. They watched from a distance as you children grew up, but your father's own smuggling activities within his gang, made it hard for the gang serving your grandparents. So your grandparents decided to pay their only visit to you, primarily to collect your brother, but also to try and convince your father to work for them. He refused on both these counts, and your grandparents were furious. It was they who caused Seth to be caught, I'm afraid to say. But the tunnels, through which Meg found her way here, connect both houses, and although we have tried to have them sealed, they continue to be reopened. So far they have never come here, and unless they get desperate, are highly unlikely to do so as Lord Sebastian would very quickly notify the authorities of their presence, and the threat they pose to you and your safety.'

`Lady Phoebe, I am so frightened. How many houses are connected by these tunnels?'

`That is a question for which I do not have an answer I'm afraid, but rest assured that when you return to Benfleet Hall, you will be much safer and far less likely to be found.'

`But what about Bartholomew and Louisa, they will still be here?'

`They will be quite safe, I give you my word. Isabella, you have to trust me on this. As I have already said, they would have to be desperate to risk coming here themselves, they are far more likely to send a lookout, or even one of Miss Amelia's Siblings. They care for no-one; all they care about is ensuring the safe arrival of their contraband. They would sacrifice anyone to avoid getting caught themselves, and to get what they want.'

`But Lady Phoebe, Bartholomew and Louisa have no sense of danger at all; they just see everything as an adventure. They would not see any risk in making a new friend and following them into a network of tunnels. This would only be a source of real excitement to them. How can we keep them safe? They even know about the secret passageway that joins my room with that of Miss Amelia. Miss Amelia was telling Louisa the story of how she first entered my room in the middle of the night, so then Louisa insisted I show her the passageway. To avoid having to do the tour twice, I took Bartholomew at the same time. Oh what have I done?'

`Hush now Isabella, their knowledge of that passageway may very well be what saves them from being kidnapped. Without realising it you have probably given them their best possible escape route, should one ever be needed. Now all is not lost, for when you return to Benfleet Hall, you will carry with you a letter from Lord Sebastian and myself, addressed to Sir Abraham and Lady Elizabeth. Contained within this letter will be the plan for your own and your family's future, I cannot say more yet, but rest assured whatever happens no harm will come to any of you, or any of us. The final part of your complete escape from your old life and, a safer, happier and more secure future is closer than you may think.'

`Oh Lady Phoebe, you and Lord Sebastian have done so much, and given so much already, we cannot accept anymore.'

`You must and you will, for it is your birthright. We can never guarantee you will not face challenges or even dangers, but you will always find the strength and wisdom to overcome them, and wherever life takes you, we are always here and will welcome you at any time. Now, we must make our way to the dining room, to join the others for dinner.'

Feeling confused, frightened, anxious and

exhausted after the emotion of this afternoon's revelations, I very much doubt whether I can eat anything, but follow Lady Phoebe through and take my place at the table. Where will life's path lead me from here? What will my future be? What lies in store for Bartholomew and Louisa?

Once again only time will tell!

Part four

It is May before the icy grip of winter finally releases its vice-like hold allowing spring, then summer to arrive. In fact it could be said that we had skipped spring this year, going straight from winter into summer. I arrived back at Benfleet Hall three months ago, having been away for almost an entire year. All four girls had grown dramatically, and the difference in Miss Ruth is the most dramatic and pleasing to see. She is now a confident, happy young woman, looking forward to a bright future and on occasions, could even be described as bossy by her three much younger sisters. This is something Sir Abraham and Lady Elizabeth feared they would never see.

Initially, it was strange and almost unreal being back here without Benedict, but I can now feel closer to him than I ever thought possible. The girls were so excited to have me back, and could not wait to tell me everything that had happened here in my absence. The last three months have really given me some hope back, although the knowledge I have of the constant, if unlikely, risk from father's family is never far from my thoughts.

***

Today I wake to find the early September sunshine streaming into my bedroom, and the scent of flowers rising up from the garden below through my open window. I rise and dress quickly heading downstairs where I can already hear voices in the dining room. The excited giggling accompanying these voices tells me that it is my three youngest students, waiting rather impatiently for breakfast to be served. As there is at least another thirty minutes before breakfast is anything like ready, I enter the dining room and suggest that they may like to join me for a short walk in the garden. This is met with little or no enthusiasm, until I tell them that their lessons today include art, and they may find something interesting or unusual to draw or paint later. Just as I am about to follow Mary, Sarah and Harriet out through the door into the dew glistening garden, Lady Elizabeth stops me.

`Isabella, may I speak with you after lunch today? It is important and concerns the letter you brought back with you when you returned to us from Havergal Manor. It is nothing to worry about, and as the girls have their music lessons this afternoon it would appear to be the most convenient time.'

I am a little shocked at this request, I had almost completely forgotten about that letter, what could be so important now?

`Why of course Lady Elizabeth, has something happened?   Is there something wrong?'

`Not at all Miss Isabella, it is just that I need to speak with you, so that plans can be made and finalised. This is necessary so that when the time comes, everything can happen in the correct order and without interference from unwanted sources.'

`Alright Lady Elizabeth, this all sounds a little unsettling and mysterious at the moment, but I will meet you in the drawing room if that is convenient?'

`I was actually thinking it may be rather nice to sit and talk either outside in the garden, or if you prefer in the garden room at the rear of the Hall, do you remember?'

A slight shiver runs through me, and a single tear escapes and runs down my cheek as I remember one previous occasion in that beautiful room that had been so joyous and happy for me only to be snatched away only a few short weeks later.

`If you wish Lady Elizabeth, it is just that it was in that room that my engagement to Benedict was announced, and I have not been able to bring myself to enter there since.'

`Oh Miss Isabella, of course please

forgive me it had quite slipped my mind, would you rather meet in the drawing room?'

Taking a deep breath, and telling myself that I cannot continue to avoid a room, especially one that had been the scene of such a happy memory, even if what has followed has tainted it somewhat.

`No Lady Elizabeth, I would like to meet in there, it is important for me to begin making new memories and not allow past events to inhibit my future.'

`Lovely, shall we say about two `o' clock then?'

`That will be fine, thank you.'

The girls have returned from the garden before I can even get a foot outside the door, so I take a few deep breaths of the sweet scented morning air, and return with the girls to the dining room.   Breakfast passes relatively quickly and peacefully, and I begin to ascend the stairs to my room to collect my lesson plans for this morning, when a small desperate voice brings me to a halt halfway up.

`Miss Isabella, could I see you for a moment please?'

It is Miss Ruth, she is standing at the bottom of the stairs looking the most distressed and anxious I have seen her for many months.

`Whatever is the matter Miss Ruth? '

By the time I reach the bottom of the stairs,

she is already in tears.

`Come child, let us take a walk in the garden and you can tell me what it is that is distressing you so.'

`Oh Miss Isabella, I could overhear you talking to Lady Elizabeth this morning, you are not leaving us again are you? You have only just come back to us, and I have missed you so much, please say you are going to stay here?'

`Miss Ruth, whatever made you think I am leaving? Lady Elizabeth just wishes to discuss a letter I brought with me when I returned, I have no knowledge of what that letter contained yet, or what it is that Lady Elizabeth wishes to discuss with me. But one thing I do know is that at the moment I am very happy to be back here with you girls. Is that all that is distressing you?'

`Well not exactly, you see when you came back your brother and sister travelled with you, didn't they?'
Slightly taken aback and very unsure where this conversation is now heading, I pause before answering.

`Bartholomew and Louisa did indeed accompany me yes, Miss Ruth. They did not want me to leave them either. Everything at Havergal Manor and their new way of life is all still very strange for them you see, and they felt afraid at the prospect of being there without me. Why?'

Her eyes look up at me with a longing and a hope that I once knew myself, and I begin to unravel Miss Ruth's question.

`Well, while you took tea with Lady Elizabeth and Miss Louisa, I could see that Master Bartholomew was looking wistfully towards the woods, so I offered to take him and show him the hidden stream, he eagerly accepted. We were not gone long because I knew we would be missed, but I did so enjoy his company, I was wondering whether if perhaps he could come for a visit here, or even perhaps I may join you when you visit Havergal Manor next time?'

Trying to suppress my mild amusement and a giggle that is desperate to escape, I decide to phrase my reply without committing to either of Miss Ruth's suggestions.

`Well now Miss Ruth, it is not I that you should be asking such a question of. If it is your wish to see Master Bartholomew, then it is your father or Lady Elizabeth whom you must discuss this with, not me. For my part I have no objection, but you must talk to either your father or Lady Elizabeth first. Do you promise me?'

`Oh must I? They do not understand me like you do Miss Isabella.'

`I think you do not give them enough credit Miss Ruth, I am sure they understand you much better than I do, and much better than you think they do. Either way you must speak to one of them before any plans can be made for such a meeting. Do you understand Miss Ruth? '

With a sigh and a look of something resembling defeat on her face, she agrees to speak to Sir Abraham.

`Now, come Miss Ruth, your sisters will be waiting, and all of you have lessons to learn.'

As we re-enter the house, my only thought is one of mild amusement as I try to imagine my often carefree, wild younger brother being tamed enough to be involved in an affair of the heart. This seems completely inappropriate in many ways, and yet the very thought of him being the object of a young girls desire is really most amusing. I cannot believe, even for a minute, that he saw their brief meeting than anything more than a walk in a wood with a girl of his own age who was just trying to be friendly and make him feel welcome. Then with a shiver, thoughts of the shadow hanging over all three of us is only too clear in my mind. How can I allow this delicate, fragile child to put herself under that same shadow? But I also know how affairs of the heart feel, who am I to get in the way of love? If indeed that is what exists between them.

Fortunately, Miss Ruth and I arrive at the school room a couple of minutes before the three younger girls, so we are ready to begin as soon as they arrive. The objects collected from the garden earlier include several brightly coloured flowers, a few leaves which are just beginning to show their jewel autumn colours, an unfortunate butterfly in a jar and several other items of flora and fauna, which when put together on a table at the front, do form a not unattractive tableau for the girls to paint or draw.

By lunchtime however, it is obvious to me that Miss Ruth is still floating somewhere with her thoughts and dreams of meeting with Bartholomew, and completely removed from reality.

`Miss Ruth, could you stay behind for a moment please? I need to ask you something important.'

`Oh, of course Miss Isabella.'

`May I see the picture which you were working on in this morning's lesson please?'

`Of course.'

To my surprise she has produced a very accomplished pencil drawing of the objects that her sisters had collected.

`This is beautiful Miss Ruth; may I take it and show your father please?'

`Must you? If he sees this he is going to want to talk to me, and then I am going to have to ask him about Bartholomew, and I do not know how too.'

Unable to suppress my amusement this time, I try to explain that even adults find some subjects hard to talk about, and that she will find the conversation much easier than her father will. She does not understand how or why this should be the case, but agrees that a discussion about her artwork will at least be an easy starting point for both of them.

Lunch is an unsettling time for me, knowing what type of conversation Miss Ruth is to have with Sir Abraham is an added concern for me, but also what could be so important that Lady Elizabeth needs to speak so urgently with me? What did that letter contain? Am I to find myself in turmoil again? Why can nothing good in my life ever last?

As arranged early this morning, I make my way to the garden room just before two o' clock. My heart is pounding as I turn the handle on the large, heavy oak door. Memories of Benedict come flooding back as my grief begins once more to consume me, this time it hits me harder than before, and as I enter the room, I am unable to breath or move from the doorway. Lady Elizabeth is already here and rushes over to my side in order to take my arm and support me.

`Miss Isabella, are you alright? Why,

whatever is the matter? Please allow me to help you.'

Once we are both seated my emotions begin to settle a little, though I am still unable to speak.

`Dear Miss Isabella, I had no idea that coming onto this room would have such a dramatic effect on you. Do you wish to take some air outside for a moment?'

Having now recovered enough breath to enable me to reply, I agree that a little walk may indeed be beneficial.

The cooling early autumn breeze gently brushing past my face is quite soothing, and I am soon feeling much calmer and more myself.

`Oh Lady Elizabeth, please forgive me, whatever must you think? I did not intend to fall apart in such a fashion, I shall be quite alright when we return, and the sweet fresh air is most soothing.'

`I am so glad, but perhaps the drawing room may be a better environment for you?'

`No, no, please do not fret or trouble yourself further, it was just the shock and all the memories returning to me, I had no idea myself that it would weaken me so. I am much improved now and ready to return, I am greatly intrigued by what you have to say to me Lady Elizabeth.'

We return to the garden room and both take a

seat allowing us to look out onto the colourful, sun-dappled garden. I can still feel my dear Benedict's presence in here, but the dread and overwhelming pain which I experienced a short while ago are less intense, and certainly appear to be easing all the time. My greatest fear now, is the uncertainty of what I am about to hear from Lady Elizabeth.

`Miss Isabella, when you returned to us three months ago you brought with you a letter, the contents of which have been kept from you until now. There are reasons for this which are unnecessary to visit at this time, but will hopefully make themselves clear to you in the near future. Now, before I explain the content of the letter, you need to understand why you are so precious to both us and Lord Sebastian and Lady Phoebe.'

This statement confuses me, and my anxiety and uncertainty begins to increase rapidly. Why am I important to Sir Abraham and Lady Elizabeth? This does not make any sense.

`Please Lady Elizabeth, I am most grateful to both you and Sir Abraham for your kindness in allowing me to play such an important role in the lives of all four girls, but why should I be precious to you? I am only a governess and tutor to your daughters and you owe me nothing.'

`Oh Miss Isabella you could not be more wrong, have you not worked everything out yet? Have you not made the link between us and Lord and Lady Havergal?'

'What do you mean? I know you are friends and that you have all shown me great kindness and compassion for which I am most grateful, but surely Lady Elizabeth that is where the connection ends?

'No Miss Isabella it is not. Benfleet Hall belongs to the Havergal estate, and Lord Sebastian is my brother. Sir Abraham's first wife, Miss Ruth's mother, was not a well woman and so when she became pregnant with Miss Ruth, Lord Sebastian gave Sir Abraham Benfleet Hall as his family had turned their backs on him because, as they saw it, he had married beneath his station. Miss Ruth's mother came from a very humble family of dubious character and although she and Sir Abraham were deeply in love, the only way they could be together was to leave their homes and come to a place where they would be left in peace and not judged by anyone. Lord Sebastian had known Sir Abraham since childhood, so he was able to give them the security they needed. Do you understand Miss Isabella?'

'I think so, but does this mean that you also knew my mother?'

I can feel the tears pricking my eyes desperate to escape, what is happening here?

'Alas yes, Lord Sebastian was older

than dear Martha, but she was the same age as I, so when we heard that you had finally made the escape to Havergal Manor Sir Abraham and I were desperate to help, but at that time we knew you needed the love and support that Lady Phoebe and Lord Sebastian were able to give you. As we had our own young family to care for, our opportunity to help came later when we needed a governess, tutor and most of all a companion for our girls, especially Miss Ruth. '

`But Lady Elizabeth, if you will permit me to enquire, how did you come to be here at Benfleet Hall? '

`Of course you may ask. Well, when dear Lady Charlotte died, Miss Ruth's Mother, her family blamed Sir Abraham for her death and wanted to take Miss Ruth to live with them. But apart from the trauma this would cause an already hurting vulnerable child, Sir Abraham knew they could not provide for a young child through legal means, and he had suspected them of smuggling and wanting to train her as a lookout for them as she got older.'

This causes me to shiver, as memories of my own childhood flash vividly into my mind.

`They then insisted that she needed a female role model, preferably a new mother before she reached the age of ten. I came here as a governess when Miss Ruth was only seven years old, but we fell in love and were married soon afterwards.'

Unable to hold them back any longer I am aware that tears are now glistening in my eyes, and now the closer I look at Lady Elizabeth, the more I can see my mother, although I know they were only cousins.

`Please Lady Elizabeth; tell me what was in the letter I brought back with me?'

`Are you alright for me to continue? This is a great deal for you to hear all in the same day.'

`I will be fine, but why did Lady Phoebe not explain all this to me before?'

`Ah, this is where the letter is important. Lady Phoebe was determined that you should come here without feeling guilty, or in any way as though we were only doing this because of who you are. The truth is we needed a governess and tutor anyway, and by giving the position to you we all felt that you would feel more prepared to accept our love and support. We were all so pleased when you and Master Benedict became engaged, and were utterly devastated when the news of his death arrived. But now you are approaching twenty-one and your brother and sister are now also safe at Havergal Manor, your future and theirs is of great importance to all of us. You are welcome to remain here as governess, tutor and companion to the girls for as long as you wish, but at some point you will need your own home and one for your sister Louisa.'

`What about Bartholomew, will he not be coming with us?'

`Well, Miss Isabella that really rather depends, as you know we have no sons of our own and were hoping that he would be prepared to come and live here with us. Dear Benedict would of course have been the natural heir, but Bartholomew is now the only heir there is ever likely to be to Benfleet Hall.' Unable to stop myself, a nervous giggle of amusement escapes through my lips.

`Oh do excuse me Lady Elizabeth, it is just that I know of at least one member of this family will be delighted by this news. Miss Ruth has rather lost her heart to my brother, after one very brief meeting, and is, at present talking to her father about the possibility of meeting him again.'

`Oh Miss Isabella, you could not be giving me better news, and I know that Sir Abraham will be delighted. He never thought that Miss Ruth would even communicate with him and us, but now to be wanting to meet with someone she has only met once is nothing short of a miracle. You have done so much, and brought so much joy here to Benfleet Hall, that when the time comes for you to leave us there will be a very large hole in all our lives.'

`I do not wish to leave Benfleet Hall or you Lady Elizabeth; I am more than content here, please tell me I can stay?'

`Of course you can stay Miss Isabella, but the girl's need of a governess will cease eventually, and then what will you do? You may meet a young man and want a home and family of your own, and when that time comes we have made provision for you. The property which my other brother Obadiah inherited called `The Croft` has not been lived in for a long time, and Obadiah has lost his right to own it, since he will inherit your grandparent's property if Bartholomew decides, as we hope he will, that he does not want it. It is our hope that he will live here at Benfleet and choose to inherit this instead.'
Fear floods my soul as a wave floods the shore in the height of a vicious storm.

`But Lady Elizabeth, if I were to live in The Croft, then surely Louisa and I would be at great risk from our father's family? I also sincerely doubt whether I could ever lose my heart to another, it will always belong to Benedict.'

`The Croft will not be yours, that place is to be sold and the money from there will help to provide you with the property that will be your home. Do you remember the large house between Havergal Manor and the farmhouse?'

`Why yes, it is a beautiful house and so surrounded by beauty also.'

`Well that is Glenville House, which is where Lady Phoebe lived as a child. As an only child she has inherited it and wishes to give it to you. You will be as safe there as you are here, and can always visit Havergal Manor and us at any time. As for never losing your heart again, do not let Benedict's loss be a barrier to you finding happiness again, he would not want that.'

`But if Lady Phoebe already owns Glenville House why does The Croft need to be sold?'

`That money is yours; it will enable you to live the life that your dear mother was so desperate for you to have Isabella, and ultimately gave her life to make it possible for you.'

`Oh Lady Elizabeth this is all too much, I cannot believe it. When must I decide?'

`There is no decision to make; it is all there waiting for you, whenever you are ready to begin the life that is rightfully yours.

Now I do believe that some tea and light refreshments would be desirable don't you?'

I gratefully agree, but my mind is still whirling from all the revelations I have heard this afternoon.

Once again in my life,
I stand at a crossroads,
Unsure of which way I should go,
Do I open the door of a future uncertain?
Turning my back on all that's familiar,
Or stay where I am,
In a place I am loved and in comfort,
But knowing my past life,
Still hovers above,
Just waiting to pounce,
At a time unexpected,
And rob me of all I have gained.

As I ascend the stairs to bed tonight my head is still so full and muddled, sleep is going to be out of the question. With this knowledge I decide to use the time to plan lessons for the girls until the end of this week, this way time will not be wasted or spent worrying about something which at the moment is to enormous to even begin to contemplate. As I enter my room, the flickering light from the lamp I am carrying begins to cast strange, dancing shadows across the walls and ceiling, and an owl screeches outside my window, causing me to almost drop the lamp. Struggling to regain my composure I place the lamp on the desk and take my seat in front of it. Having managed to calm my nerves I am now ready to begin my lesson planning for the rest of the week.

It is already well after midnight and I have only just managed to crawl into bed, with my eyes so heavy I decide that I must at least try and get some sleep, or I will not be able to use the plans which I have been working so hard on tonight. My eyes refuse to stay open, but my mind is refusing to stop. As I lay here in the velvet darkness with only the occasional owl interrupting the calm, tranquil silence of the early autumn night, I can at last begin to see things more clearly.   Lady Elizabeth is quite correct in saying that I am going to need a home of my own, where Louisa and I can live and be happy looking forward to a future filled with hope. But what will happen when Louisa finds love and desires to marry, am I to remain in that house alone for the rest of my days. My mind flashes back to the line in my dear Benedict's final letter to me;

`**My final prayer is that you will meet someone who can give you that which I have not been able too, and you must never feel guilty about giving your most precious gift of love to another who makes you feel special and secure. Your future happiness is what I long for. '**

This most sincere, heartfelt and passionate

desire has now been echoed on two separate occasions. The first of these being by Lady Phoebe on the day I returned to Havergal Manor last year following my father's funeral, the very same day that I received that letter. The second of these came only today, when Lady Elizabeth suggested that perhaps I may yet lose my heart again to some gentleman whom to date I have not met. It is with these thoughts going through my mind that I eventually drift off to sleep. These same thoughts are still in my mind this morning as I prepare for the day's lessons, but are soon forgotten when an extremely excited Miss Ruth practically chases me downstairs for breakfast.

`Oh Miss Isabella, Miss Isabella, you just could not believe how wonderful my life has become in only the last two days. Father is so wonderful and I feel as though I could skip and jump for ever.'

`Whatever has got you so excited Miss Ruth? I have never seen you this way before, I am used to your sisters getting giddy and talkative, but I did not expect to see such behaviour from you! Now calm yourself and tell me what is so momentous that you have completely lost all sense of propriety.'

`Oh Miss Isabella, please do not be cross, I do not mean to behave like an unruly child, but it is thanks to you that my life has changed so much and just keeps getting better and better.'

Trying very hard to suppress my own amusement and mild excitement, I take several deep breaths before attempting to reply in a calm and lady-like fashion. For deep down I already know some of what has caused Miss Ruth to behave in such a way.

`I am not cross Miss Ruth, but one must remember that young ladies are expected to behave in a certain way and observe the etiquette that this entails. Now without jumping about like an excited puppy, perhaps you would like to tell me your news.'

`Miss Isabella, I would first like to thank you for encouraging me to talk to my father yesterday, far from being angry with me and against any further meetings between myself and Bartholomew, he actually said he would be delighted to welcome him here. He also agreed that I could accompany you to Havergal Manor next weekend, providing that is acceptable to you. Please say I can come with you? '

`Of course you may come with me, I should be delighted to have your company, and Miss Louisa would also enjoy seeing you again, I am sure. Did your father say anything else Miss Ruth?'

A look of surprise appears on the heart-shaped face with piecing grey-green eyes that is looking up at me.

`Well, actually Miss Isabella he did, but how did you know? Anyway, that is not important, the best news is that father intends to ask Master Bartholomew to come and live here eventually, and has said that a union between the two of us would be most desirable for all concerned. But now I am nervous Miss Isabella, what happens if Master Bartholomew does not return my affection? I fear my heart may break if I were to be rebuffed.'

`Now Miss Ruth, there is no reason to be melodramatic, we will not know Master Bartholomew's own feelings until we arrive at Havergal Manor next weekend. He has never before known young ladies of his own age, so may appear shy and insecure at first, but I do not think that you have too much to fear, and as for your heart breaking, I think that is highly unlikely. Now we must join the others for breakfast, and please try not to excite your sisters too much, you all still have lessons to learn and attend too today alright?'

`Yes Miss Isabella, I am so happy that you came back to us, I just know we will be friends forever.'

`Of course we will, and even when we may not be together, friendship will continue to unite us Miss Ruth.'

The look of concern on her face when I say

this really touches my heart, but she seems reassured when I explain to her that whatever happens, visits in both directions will be a regular occurrence.

All four girls apply themselves really well to their lessons this morning, and lunchtime arrives almost too quickly. In fact they are so eager to complete their work that I have to agree to them returning early this afternoon so that they are able to complete this morning's work before starting their tasks for the afternoon. This is a source of great encouragement to me and I know that their need for me still exists, and will continue to do so for some time to come. But I also know that Miss Louisa needs me to be her sister, and that being separated from her whilst I fulfil my duties here at Benfleet Hall, cannot be allowed to continue for much longer. Once again my loyalties are being tested, and torn in different directions, and I now realise that I must speak to Lady Phoebe about Glenville House when I visit Havergal Manor next weekend.

***

The last week and a half have been uneventful yet fulfilling. The attitudes of the girls to their lessons are now so good that I am struggling to plan enough work to keep them interested and occupied, I am also beginning to feel that they will soon have more knowledge than I, and will be able to teach me things. This weekend I am to visit Havergal Manor for the first time since my return to Benfleet Hall to recommence my duties here. Miss Ruth is to travel with me on this occasion, as she desires to spend time with Master Bartholomew. I need to check on both Master Bartholomew and Miss Louisa, to ascertain how well or not, they have adapted to their new life. It is also important that I spend time with Miss Louisa particularly, so that she knows her sister has not forgotten or abandoned her. She is still only twelve years old, and therefore a child who needs to feel love, reassurance and comfort. I must say I will be glad to have company on this occasion, as I know I have to talk to Lady Phoebe about Glenville House, and ultimately when she feels would be the right time for Miss Louisa and myself to make our move to what is to be my permanent home, and Miss Louisa's for as long as she wants or needs to be there.

The magnitude of the decision which ultimately I will have to make is resting heavily on my shoulders at this time. It is for this reason my talk with Lady Phoebe is so important this weekend, it is not a decision which I feel capable of making alone, or at the very least without the advice of someone whom I know and love dearly, as well as trust implicitly. My entire future and that of my young sister is dependent on this decision. It will also vastly affect the lives of another family whom I have grown to love very dearly, those living at Benfleet Hall. Of all those who live there it is my travelling companion this weekend, whom I fear for the most. Miss Ruth has been through so much in her young life, and she is now really blossoming into a confident and happy young woman. Even when I was absent for nearly a year she had the hope and near certain knowledge of my return. But when I make this, my final and most significant move it will be for good, and I fear that when she realises this, and any hope of me returning is taken from her, that she will regress and once again close herself off from the world. My only glimmer of hope that this will not happen, is her new found interest in eventually forming a union with my brother, Master Bartholomew. I only hope he responds favourably towards her, and that her feelings are reciprocated.

***

Today is bright and still pleasantly warm for the time of year, with a gentle breeze blowing barely moving the jewel-coloured leaves enough to provide percussion to accompany the birdsong that seems to be filling the air with its enchanting melody. It will be a pleasant journey for myself and Miss Ruth today as we travel to Havergal Manor for the weekend. Miss Ruth is bubbling over with sheer excitement and the thrill of being away from home for the first time in her life, as well as with the knowledge that she will soon be seeing Master Bartholomew again. For me on the other hand this journey is causing very mixed emotions, as my entire future, and that of my sister rests on the discussion to be had, and decisions to be made this weekend. I can already feel my stomach knotting up inside as the carriage begins its journey away from Benfleet Hall. How can I possibly leave all this and the family dwelling here behind? But how can I deny myself and my sister the future and the life that our mother was so eager for us to have and enjoy?

Our journey begins in silence as Miss Ruth appears to be enchanted at the beautifully picturesque scenery we are passing, but this does not last for long.

`Oh Miss Isabella, this is so exciting isn't it? I cannot wait to get there, and see Master Bartholomew again. What is Havergal Manor like?'

`Calm yourself Miss Ruth; I know this is all a new experience for you but you must not expect too much from Master Bartholomew on only your second meeting.

Havergal Manor is beautiful, especially at this time of year, and I understand from speaking with Lady Elizabeth this morning, that Lady Phoebe cannot wait to meet and welcome you. But we must remember how young ladies are expected to behave and conduct themselves mustn't we? This is especially important in the company of strangers, propriety and etiquette must be observed at all times.'

`I am sorry Miss Isabella, I will behave acceptably I promise, but what do you mean by not expecting too much from Master Bartholomew? And why is Lady Phoebe so keen to meet me?'

`I know you will not let me or yourself down Miss Ruth. With regards to Master Bartholomew, he is a shy young man who is not used to being the centre of anyone's attention, least of all that of a young lady. He may appear to be aloof and withdrawn to begin with, so you will have to be patient and understanding with him if your friendship is to develop into something more, do you think you can give him the time and space that he will need?'

Looking puzzled, Miss Ruth does not answer this question immediately, but instead she is gazing out of the carriage window watching a buzzard that is circling high above us in the cloudless clear blue sky.

`Are you alright Miss Ruth? You have become very quiet and thoughtful.'

`I am fine Miss Isabella, and I really do love Master Bartholomew, if he needs time and space then of course I will give it to him, why did you think I wouldn't?'
The hurt in her voice is obvious.

`I did not mean to hurt or offend you, I am glad you feel that way and knowing you as well as I do, I should not have doubted you. But you must understand that Master Bartholomew is my brother so is very special to me, I could not bear to see him get hurt. Will you accept my sincere apology Miss Ruth?'

A cheerful though more subdued smile than usual returns to her face, and my concern for her remains.

`Of course I forgive you Miss Isabella, but I am feeling nervous and afraid now, I do not think I am going to know what to say to him. Will you introduce us again formally Miss Isabella?'
Trying hard to suppress a giggle, and not let my mild amusement at her sudden change of demeanour show, I take a deep breath before I attempt to reply.

`Of Course, if you wish me too, but remember he too will be nervous so just be yourself and try to allow things to happen and develop naturally.'

The carriage begins to slow as we approach the large wrought iron gates at the end of the long gravel drive to Havergal Manor, and as we turn in through these gates, the knot in my stomach tightens and Miss Ruth grips my arm tightly.

`What is it Miss Ruth? What is wrong?'

`Oh Miss Isabella, I can hardly breathe, I am excited and scared all at the same time, you will stay with me won't you? I could not cope with being somewhere new and being on my own!'

`Of course I shall remain with you. You are in my care whilst we are away from Benfleet Hall, but let me assure you that there is nothing for you to fear, everybody here will love you as much as I do.'

`Oh do you really, truly, love me Miss Isabella? Do you really think that everyone else here will love me too? Why should they? They have never met me; they do not know me at all!'

`You are very easy to love Miss Ruth, and they will all want to get to know you so that they can love you too. Do not fret child, by the time we make our return to Benfleet Hall tomorrow afternoon, you will wonder why you ever panicked so. You will feel as at home and relaxed here as you do in your own home.'

The horses begin draw to a halt, and Lord

Sebastian is here to greet us as we alight from the carriage.

`Welcome back Miss Isabella, and please allow me to offer a most warm welcome to you Miss Ruth. We are delighted that you have come to pay us a visit so that we might finally get to know you personally, after everything that Miss Isabella and Master Bartholomew have told us about you, to make your acquaintance at last is a great honour.'

`Thank you Lord Sebastian, I am most honoured to meet you too. What has Master Bartholomew been saying?'
I too am surprised by this piece of news; maybe my fears about Master Bartholomew's reaction to being the focus of a young lady's attention are quite misplaced.

`Master Bartholomew has not stopped talking about the time he spent with you when he travelled to Benfleet Hall with Miss Isabella three months ago. He has been at great pains to explain how you went out of your way to make him feel welcome and at ease, and is delighted that you have come to stay with us this weekend.'

`Oh Miss Isabella, did you hear that? He wants to see me; this is just the most wonderful news ever. My life is so perfect today that I never want this day to end.'

`Now Miss Ruth, remember what we talked about on our journey here today.'

`Yes Miss Isabella, I remember, and I will try my best, it is just that I never thought I would feel like this, and it is so wonderfully exciting.'

Lord Sebastian smiles knowingly at me, before leading us both in doors and towards the drawing room, here Lady Phoebe, Miss Amelia and Miss Louisa are all waiting for us to arrive and take tea with them.

`Good afternoon Lady Phoebe, may I present Miss Ruth.'

`Delighted to meet you Miss Ruth, this is Miss Amelia, and Miss Louisa you have already met of course.'

`It is an honour for me to meet you all and thank you so much for allowing me to visit and stay with you this weekend.'

`You are most welcome child. Now both of you come in and sit down. I am sure that some tea and light refreshment will be most welcome after your journey, however pleasant the weather may be today.'

`Thank you Lady Phoebe, I am sure I can speak for both Miss Ruth and myself when I say that we would appreciate that greatly.'

`Miss Ruth will be staying in Miss Louisa's room if that is acceptable to her? Miss Louisa was so glad you were coming this weekend Miss Ruth and immediately requested that you be allowed to share her room.'

`That will be most acceptable, thank you Lady Phoebe. I was so dreading being alone at night in a strange place, so this is a great relief to me.'

`Good, then that is settled, when you have had sufficient refreshment Miss Louisa will show you up to your room for the night, and then you may accompany her out into the garden if you wish.'

`Thank you again Lady Phoebe that would be lovely.'

Miss Ruth and Miss Louisa waste no time in taking their leave, and in spite of her initial protestations Miss Amelia is despatched to keep an eye on them. I know that this is because Lady Phoebe wishes to speak with me alone, but the temptation to excuse myself too, so that I can ensure Miss Ruth is alright, is very great at the moment. I do not want to have this conversation, yet have it I must and the sooner the better, or it could cast a heavy shadow over the entire weekend.

`Miss Isabella, you are looking so much better since you returned to your duties at Benfleet Hall. Has it provided you with the focus and routine that you felt you so badly needed?'

`It most certainly has Lady Phoebe, and all four girls are such a delight to teach. They are all very eager to learn, and in fact my main problem now, is not so much how best to encourage enthusiasm, but how to plan enough work to keep them all fully occupied for the duration of each lesson. I must ask you though, how well have Bartholomew and Louisa adapted to their life here at Havergal Manor? Do they appear to have settled in successfully?'

`I can assure you Isabella there are no concerns about either of them in that direction. Both are adapting extremely well and are even enjoying their lessons now.'
This is said with slight amusement showing in Lady Phoebe's voice, as she and I both remember how unfair they considered life to be when they first arrived here and discovered they were to be taught lessons on a daily basis.

Realising I have neither seen or heard my brother since my arrival here this afternoon, nearly an hour ago, I become concerned.

`Lady Phoebe where is Master Bartholomew this afternoon?'

`He has gone riding with Thomas, but as soon as he returns, it is my belief that he will want to see Miss Ruth.'

`Yes, Lord Sebastian indicated when we arrived that he had not stopped talking about her since they met three months hence.'

`That is true, he seems to be extremely

taken with her, I only hope she will not be put off by his rather romantic advances.'

`Miss Ruth will most certainly not be put off; in fact I believe I can guarantee that she will be absolutely delighted. She has been holding a light for him since their brief meeting too. This is the reason she has chosen to accompany me here this weekend.'

Both Lady Phoebe and I find ourselves most amused by this set of circumstances, and for the first time I begin to relax. I know that the inevitable, important discussion must take place this afternoon, but strangely the fear of it is leaving me, being replaced by a new and certain hope of a future that has been planned for me since childhood. My dear mother sacrificed her happiness and ultimately her life to make this possible, and now it is really happening, I just wish that she had been able to see her plan come into being before her time on earth was cut so cruelly short. Louisa and I must now embrace this opportunity at the right time and then not look back.

Mother your plan is now real,
Our lives have been changed for the good,
The life that you only dreamed of,
Will be ours,
But at such a great cost.
The love that we shared between us,
I know can never be lost,

But oh how I wish you could be here,
To see the joy we now have and enjoy,
And witness the spirit of family,
Surrounding us all like a flood.

`Dearest Isabella, I understand from Lady Elizabeth that you are already aware of a large proportion of the letter that you took back with you when you returned to Benfleet Hall, but what you may not be aware of is that Glenville House comes with its own title. When you reach the age of twenty-one in February next year, you will have the right to become Lady Glenville and as soon as you are ready after that date, the property and title are yours for life. Should you marry and have children, then it will automatically pass to them, if you are not fortunate enough to be blessed this way, then Miss Louisa will inherit, followed by any children she may have. If you do find the right young man to give your heart too and marry, the property and the title will still be yours. Do you understand all that I am saying to you?'

`I believe I do Lady Phoebe, but if Glenville House is your inheritance, then surely you are Lady Glenville, that is your right?'

`If I had not married Lord Sebastian then you would be quite correct, but although it is my inheritance, as soon as I married I assumed my husband's name and therefore shared in his title, so you see Isabella I have no need for it. This is my gift to you and will go some way to putting right the wrong from all those years ago.'

`But Lady Phoebe, yourself and Lord Sebastian have done so much for me and my family already, there is surely no further debt to be paid?'

`Isabella, I have no use for such a place, or the title that goes with it, and you do have such a need. It is for this reason I desire you to have it and love it as I know you will. All my memories from my childhood spent there are happy ones, so I know that your life there will also be happy. If for any reason you feel in danger or at risk at any time, the journey back to here is not a long one, and as a birthday present to you, we have decided that you should have your own horse so that you are able to enjoy the beautiful countryside that surrounds Glenville house. I assume you are able to ride Isabella? '

Feeling stunned and overwhelmed, I am unable answer immediately, but realise that the very few times I sat on Fergus our terribly old pony as an extremely young child, hardly constitute a proven ability in the saddle.

`Well Lady Phoebe, the only times I have been on horseback in my life were as a very young child when I was allowed to ride our very elderly pony called Fergus. He died when I was only ten and I am ashamed to say that I have not ridden since.'

`Well then it is high time you learnt to ride properly, and as your mare is already living in our stables, why don't we take a walk down there so you can meet her?'

Suddenly remembering what Lady Phoebe had said earlier about Master Bartholomew, I feel encouraged and agree.

`Thank you Lady Phoebe, I would love to be able to ride, I assume that both Master Bartholomew and Miss Louisa have already learnt?'

`They have indeed, and both are now happy and confident in the saddle. Miss Louisa often accompanies Miss Amelia on her early morning ride, and Master Bartholomew loves nothing more than escaping with Thomas every afternoon for a gallop across the fells.'

`But Lady Phoebe is his eyesight sufficiently good for him to be able to see well enough to be safe while moving at speed on horseback in the open countryside?'

`Oh Isabella, I should have told you, since your brother has had his spectacles and his diet has improved, his eyesight is much improved also. He is really beginning to flourish, and is a much more confident and happy young man than the one who arrived here and you left behind when you returned to Benfleet Hall.'

`Oh Lady Phoebe, that is such good news, I have always been concerned that he would be unable to live an independent and fulfilled life. But I see now that these fears have all been quite unnecessary. We all owe you and Lord Sebastian so much, how can we ever repay such an enormous debt of gratitude?'

`You owe us nothing Isabella; it was our duty to atone for the great wrong that your mother suffered at the hands of your great uncle. This has been such an honour and a privilege to be able to put things right, fulfil dear Martha's dying wish and see you all flourish as your lives change so dramatically for the better.'

As we arrive at the stables, Thomas and Bartholomew are just returning from their latest adventure, and for the first time in years, my brother has colour in his cheeks and the look of someone who is now really enjoying life to the full.

`Good afternoon Miss Isabella, are you well?'

`Quite well thank you Master Thomas, and yourself?'

`Perfectly well thank you. It is a great pleasure to see you again.'

`You too, thank you so much for taking

my brother under your wing, I really am most appreciative of what you have done for him in my absence.'

`It has been a pleasure Miss Isabella; I am really enjoying having some younger male company to do things with.'

`Well Master Bartholomew, have you enjoyed your ride this afternoon?'

`Oh yes Isabella, I really enjoy it every afternoon, it is so exciting and exhilarating. How long have you been here? I must get back to the house and get cleaned up before I meet Miss Ruth.'

`You always did have an adventurous spirit, but you were never one for being clean and tidy. We arrived about two hours ago, and Miss Ruth is quite contentedly spending time with Miss Amelia and Miss Louisa at present, so there is no reason for you to rush away. I have not seen you for three months either.'

The look of shock and disappointment that passes across my brother's face has to be seen to be believed, and I have to fight hard to contain my amusement.

`Oh I am sorry Isabella, it is just that I really want to make the right impression as my future happiness depends on this weekend. I have great respect for Miss Ruth and I really want her to love me as much as I love her. A day does not go by when I do not think of her beauty and welcoming heart. '

`I was only teasing you, off you go and I am sure you will not be disappointed.'

As I look at Lady Phoebe, I can see that she too sensed my brother's impatience to get away from his sister, and find the young lady who has quite obviously stolen his heart.

As soon as I set my eyes on Venus, I fall for her placid nature and quiet temperament, and I long to be able to ride her with the same confidence that I have just witnessed in my brother.

`Oh Lady Phoebe she is beautiful, when can I ride her?'

`Well, why don't you and Miss Ruth join the other two girls tomorrow morning and see how you get on? I am sure that we can find a suitable mount for her. '

`Well I cannot speak for Miss Ruth; I will have to ask her. But as for me, I would love to. I just hope I do not slow them down, or fall off and make a fool of myself.'

`I am sure that will not happen Isabella, Miss Amelia is a very experienced and accomplished horse woman, and will help and encourage you all the way. I will make sure that you both have suitable attire to go riding in before you retire to bed tonight.'

***

My first ride early this morning was beautiful, and despite my initial anxiety and misgivings the freedom I felt in the saddle, on the back of Venus was immense. By the time I return to Havergal Manor just before breakfast my mind is made up. The decision I thought was going to be so hard and traumatic, has quite suddenly been made so easy for me. It is almost as though it has been taken completely out of my hands and made for me with such clarity and definition that I know without any doubt or fear it is the right thing to do, both for myself and Miss Louisa. The pure joy that radiated through her this morning while we were riding together, and since we have returned, through her excited conversation has confirmed everything for me. Now that my mind is made up and I know what I must do, I will speak with Lady Phoebe this morning.

Breakfast passes quietly and uneventfully, and for the first time in many months there is a very real sense of hope, satisfaction and fulfilment rising up within me. Even my concerns regarding leaving Miss Ruth behind, have been greatly eased, she has been so happy to be able to spend time with Master Bartholomew that she has barely noticed my presence this entire weekend. I am also thrilled to see my brother so happy and able to engage so freely with a comparative stranger. This is something I doubted would ever happen, but his confidence has grown so much since his arrival here at Havergal Manor, and I know that much of this is down to the time he has spent with Thomas. I owe him a lot, and will be able to thank him now without feeling threatened or ill at ease when I am in his presence, even if we are alone.

Knowing that Miss Ruth and I are to return to Benfleet Hall after lunch, I can see that Lady Phoebe is making ready to leave the breakfast table, so I also excuse myself and follow her from the dining room.

`Lady Phoebe I must speak with you before we leave this afternoon, when would be the best time please?'

Smiling gently but knowingly, she turns towards me before making her reply.

`Would you like to take a walk in the garden with me now Isabella? We can talk freely and shall not be disturbed out there.'

`Thank you Lady Phoebe, I would appreciate that, and the garden is so idyllically serene and peaceful I immediately feel at ease and a really powerful sense of well-being.'

`I know just what you mean Isabella. '
As we leave the confines of the house behind us, and make our way across the lawn, Lady Phoebe continues.

`You have come to a decision haven't you Isabella? I do know it cannot have been easy for you, but it is my hope that coming back here this weekend has helped a little.'

'Oh Lady Phoebe, coming back here yesterday, I was filled with such a mix of emotions, but as soon as I arrived and saw how settled and happy Miss Louisa and later Master Bartholomew were, I knew we were all in the right place.'

'Does this mean that you are not going to take up residency at Glenville House after all?'

'On the contrary Lady Phoebe, that definitely is not the case. While I was out riding this morning the decision I had to make became so clear, and felt so right, that I wanted to speak to you urgently. I would dearly love to take up residency at Glenville House with Miss Louisa as soon as possible after Christmas. If that is acceptable, with you and Lord Sebastian?'

'Miss Isabella we would be delighted, and fully understand that you would want to spend Christmas in familiar surroundings. Will that be here with your brother and sister, or at Benfleet Hall?'

'Well actually Lady Phoebe, I believe that both Master Bartholomew and Miss Ruth would dearly love to spend it together, and I would dearly love to spend this Christmas with both of my siblings. I intend to speak with Lady Elizabeth on our return to Benfleet Hall this afternoon, and ask her whether it would be possible for both Miss Louisa and Master Bartholomew to spend Christmas with me at Benfleet Hall. I do hope that you will not be offended by this?'

`Dearest Isabella, I think that would be a wonderful idea, and of course we are not offended. It is vital that you all spend as much time as a family as you can, meanwhile I will make all the necessary arrangements for your arrival at Glenville House, both with the staff there and by ensuring the safe delivery of all your possessions that are not with you at Benfleet Hall. Miss Louisa's belonging will also be delivered ready for your arrival. I know you will both be very happy there, and grow to love it as much as I do.'

Decision made, it is as though an enormous cloud has broken above me, and a new dawn is just about to appear on the horizon. Finally all three of us can begin to look forward to a brighter and more positive future, or at least have the very real hope of one.

We can finally start our lives afresh,
No longer entangled in the smuggler's mesh,
Though threats from our past,
Like clouds may still hover,
And their evil may cast,
A shadow like cover,
The brightest of hope,
Will break through this power,

Giving us all the strength to cope,
With no longer any need to cower.

***

Today is the third day of April, and unlike last year winter's grip is already fading quickly, the blossom is beginning to adorn the trees with a regal splendour which is unrivalled at any other time of the year. I am still residing at Benfleet Hall and continuing to undertake my duties as governess and tutor all four girls. Master Bartholomew and Miss Louisa are here with me as for the first time in many years, we were able to spend Christmas as a family. Until the weather breaks fully they will remain here as I will, so I also have to oversee their tuition which is very hard for them and me as they do not like being taught by their big sister so the atmosphere as well as our relationship can be strained at times. But this situation will not remain for much longer now, as each new day brings further improvement in the weather. However, this year I will not be returning to Havergal Manor as Miss Louisa and I, are to take up ownership and residency of Glenville House, and begin our new lives there. Master Bartholomew will be returning to Havergal Manor, although his time is to be split between there and Benfleet Hall, as the love that he and Miss Ruth share is continuing to grow and flourish. The visits that Miss Louisa and I will be paying to both Benfleet Hall and Havergal Manor will be as regular and frequent as we can make them, as both places and more especially the people residing in them are very special to me, and I suspect to Miss Louisa.

Our arrival at Glenville House is planned for the first week of May, and as this deadline approaches my feelings and emotions are tumultuously mixed. This does not negatively affect the hope that is welling up inside me however. A hope which I never thought possible, and which has only been made possible after a series of traumatic and tragic events beginning with my dear mother's premature demise, and culminating in the prolonged, harrowing, yet freedom-giving demise of my cruel father, whom I had lived in fear of for many years, even after I had arrived into the safety and love of Havergal Manor.

At the tender age of just fifteen I was already living a life of drudgery, fear and poverty, but now just six years later, at the age of twenty-one, I am about to take ownership of my own property and the title which accompanies it. I am beginning an adventure in my life I could once have only dreamed of. My beautiful horse and companion Venus has been stabled at Benfleet

Hall since late October, and until the weather closed in so hard that we could not go anywhere, I rode her regularly every morning and evening. During which time I discovered that I was in fact most content in the saddle with the freedom and exhilaration which this activity gave me. Either Miss Louisa or Miss Ruth joined me most mornings, but as they were both needing to ride Comet, Miss Louisa's chestnut gelding, because Miss Ruth did not yet own her own horse, this could be challenging. Master Bartholomew did offer his back stallion on loan to Miss Ruth, but it was soon very obvious that he was far too strong for her to control.

***

I wake this morning to find the early spring sunshine streaming through my window, and when I get up and look out at the garden below, instead of the last of winter's snow and frost, there is fresh green grass bejeweled with diamond-like dewdrops. With the thrill and excitement of a ten year old child on her birthday, I dress quickly in my riding clothes for the first time this year, and head without delay to the stables, not waiting for anyone to accompany me. For some reason this morning I need to be alone with my thoughts. The sweet spring air begins to refresh every part of me, and as soon as Venus catches sight of me approaching her stable, she begins to whinny with excitement and delight that rivals my own. I am met with bemusement and curiosity by the stable hand Mordecai, who, instead of greeting me in his usual friendly manner, appears concerned, not to say disturbed by my uncharacteristic exuberant enthusiasm.

`Do you want to ride this morning Miss? The ground is still quite hard with this chill in the air.'

`I am indeed wishing to ride, please will you be good enough to get Venus ready for me, I need to feel the freedom of the wind rushing through my hair, that I have missed so much over the course of the long dark winter.'

`Are you going out alone Miss? Should you not wait for a companion?'

`Please do not worry yourself, I shall be perfectly alright, I just need to be alone so that I may fully appreciate this wonderful gift, the gift of this glorious morning.'

`Very well Miss.'

While I wait for Venus to be ready, I am absorbed by a tiny wren singing clearly and sweetly as she sits on a blossom shrouded bough high above my head. I am not kept waiting long, and Venus stands calmly and serenely whilst I get myself up into the saddle.

As I set off on my early morning ride

however the atmosphere changes. There is now a heaviness that I have not felt before and Venus my five year old grey mare seems to become unsettled. This is unusual because she has such a placid nature. We have been out for no more than ten minutes when, with no warning Venus rears up violently and I am thrown. She bolts and is out of sight before I have recovered myself enough to fully realise what is happening. Whatever has startled her is a mystery but my focus is now on finding her. My thoughts return to Mordecai and his concern as I left the stable yard a few short minutes ago, did he already feel a tension which I did not?

I continue through the woods and out into the fields beyond, it is a route I know well, only this morning I feel uneasy, as though I am encroaching into a private world. Alone and isolated the old farmhouse now looks even more sinister as the early morning mist swirls around obscuring parts of it and revealing others. The bleak landscape that surrounds me and this house does nothing to ease my anxiety and increasing feeling of being watched. This place has not been lived in for years, but now there are signs of someone making this ramshackle old building into their home. Why would anyone want to live here? Who would chose a derelict building? A shiver runs through me, I do not know why, but although my instinct is telling me to turn and run, something is drawing me closer. The only sound is a huge black bird circling above me screeching continuously.

***

Secret passages underground,
Meetings in the dark,
United in a common cause,
Guilty though they were.
Gentlemen with secret lives
Looking to secure,
Earnings and financial gain,
Running risks at every turn.
Smuggling was their game.

Dear Reader
If you have enjoyed reading this book, then
please leave a review on Amazon.
Thank you.

About the Author

Elizabeth Manning-Ives is the pen name of published poet Helen Thwaites and `Living Under the Shadow` is Elizabeth's debut novel. As well as writing, Helen also enjoys a variety of handicrafts, nature and playing the flute. In the past she has also been involved with many local am-dram productions. She is heavily involved with her church where she currently enjoys the challenge of helping with youth work on Sunday mornings. She loves chocolate and insists that it stimulates and enhances her writing.

To find out more about Elizabeth or to follow her on social media visit
https://livingundertheshadow76.wordpress.com/